ZANE

The K9 Files, Book 3

Dale Mayer

Books in This Series:

ZANE: THE K9 FILES, BOOK 3
Dale Mayer
Valley Publishing Ltd.

ISBN-13: 978-1-773361-53-6
Print Edition

About This Book

Going home wasn't part of his plan …

Agreeing to travel home to Maine to hunt down Katch, a K9 dog the system had lost track of, wasn't an easy decision for Zane. It meant facing his drunk of a father, his cold older brother and, worst of all, Holly, his kid brother's widow—who used to be his girlfriend.

Finding Katch looked to be the easiest part of this dysfunctional homecoming. Only he wasn't the only one hunting Katch.

Holly has been through a whirlwind of emotions in the last few years. But the good thing in all of this was the hope that Zane would finally come home again. They had a history to clear up and a future to forge … she hoped.

A call for help brings the injured shepherd to Holly's doorstep, plus a hunter looking to finish what he started. All thoughts of a future with Zane are threatened now and forever as the hunter decides two-legged prey are just as good as four-legged ones.

Sign up to be notified of all Dale's releases here!

http://dalemayer.com/category/blog/

PROLOGUE

EVEN AS PIERCE stared in disbelief as the votes came in—giving him the job of the sheriff in Arrowhead, Colorado—back in New Mexico, Zane Carmichael sat down at Badger's desk and said, "I hear searching for some dogs is going on."

Badger shifted back in his chair, steepled his fingers and studied Zane. "Do you have any K9 experience?"

"No," he said. "Artillery IEDs, all kinds of military experience, but nothing with dogs. On the other hand, I was raised with them, and I'd say I have a talent for them too."

Badger's eyebrows pulled together. "Tell me more."

"Animals of all kinds speak to me," he said. "It's just easier for me than for a lot of people. I've had basic dog obedience training but not the high-level training of K9 handlers."

"Here's what we've got so far," Badger said and spent ten minutes sorting through what they'd done to date.

"I know Ethan and Pierce both had K9 training," Zane said. "I'd like to try though."

"We have ten dogs left to locate," Badger said. "The top of the pack was lost at the airport in Bangor, Maine. His last confirmed location was Stetson, Maine."

"Stetson?" Zane frowned. "How about any other place but there?"

"Why is that?"

"I've got family back in Maine, just outside of Corinna," he said. "Holly, my younger brother's widow, is somebody I'm trying to avoid."

"Why?" Badger asked.

Zane gave him a lopsided glance. "I cared too much. Brody's widow was my ex-girlfriend. After my baby brother passed away, I went home for the funeral but left as soon as I could. Holly was leaning on me too much, as if wanting me to step into my brother's shoes, and that was the last thing I wanted," Zane said bluntly. "I'd like to be loved for myself, not because I'm a reflection of another man."

"Wow," Badger said. "Sounds like you need to get back to Maine then. And ... Gunner gave Titanium Corp a sizable donation, particularly to fund the War Dogs searches. So your expenses will all be covered." He picked up the file. "I've got a younger male here called Katch." He frowned at the name. "He's well-known for his ability to catch, apparently." He studied the first page. "He was sent home after not following commands well enough under fire. He ended up with PTSD after one particularly bad bombing, and they couldn't get him to function properly afterward. He was returned to a training compound, then shipped out to an adopted family. He was lost at the airport, and the adopted family never got him. He showed up in Bangor, and we were alerted, but nobody could catch him. Our last notification said he was picked up by a hunter. Considering Katch is suffering from PTSD, that could be problematic. Now we're not sure where he is. Last known sighting was Stetson."

"Dammit." Zane studied the stack of files. "You sure you don't want to give me one of the others—a long way away from Maine?"

"Just for that reason alone," Badger said, leaning forward, "sounds to me like Maine it is. If you're ready …" He picked up the file and tossed it at him. "Katch."

CHAPTER 1

"MAINE?" ZANE SHUDDERED and sank deeper into his airline seat. "Why couldn't it be anywhere else but Maine?"

The old lady beside him twittered. "Maine is a lovely place. I don't know what you have against it," she quietly sang out in her light birdlike voice. "I can't wait to get home."

He cast her a sideways glance and gave her a goofy grin. "I'm from Maine, so it's all good."

"No, it's not," she said. "For whatever reason, you're having trouble with the idea. And you should let it go, young man. Life's too short to worry about everything, and going to Maine is definitely not one of the things you should worry about."

"It's just that I'll have to face some people I don't really want to face," he tried to explain. "Well, one in particular. One who I used to really like, and I'm hoping I don't anymore."

She looked at him in confusion, then a crafty gleam entered her eyes. "Ah, a girlfriend? Sounds like maybe it's time to go back and to make peace with yourself. You can't go forward if you have baggage holding you back."

He chuckled. "Don't you worry. I can handle it."

"Hogwash," she retorted. "I might be old, but I'm not

senile. And the young always think they have all the answers. Instead they just keep shoving away the questions and never getting to the *real* answers." She settled back into her seat, raising her book to eye level.

He looked at the cover and grinned because it was a romance novel. To him it was incongruous, and yet, there was no reason for her either to not have her own romance or to take pleasure in reading about someone else's romance. When had he become scared of romance? Likely when his ex-girlfriend had married his kid brother.

He stared out the window, realizing they'd descend soon. He pulled out his phone and checked for messages. Before heading to his last connecting flight, he'd sent yet another text to Badger. **Seriously, a one-way ticket to Maine?**

Badger's response had been instant. **Absolutely. Maine for you.**

So Zane was heading to Bangor first, then driving toward Stetson, which was the last known point where the dog Katch had been picked up by a hunter. Although, in the last few days, it was possible the hunter no longer had the dog. Its whereabouts after that were unknown. Zane's hometown of Newport was close enough to use as a base. Zane said aloud, "Maybe the dog is happy there."

"You better not be talking about a girlfriend," the old lady warned in that birdlike voice. "That's no way to talk about a young lady."

"I'm talking about a dog," he explained. "I'm tracking down a War Dog who served in Afghanistan but then ended up with PTSD after too many bombings."

"Why do you think he's in trouble?"

"Because we got a notice that the dog had potentially

hooked up with a hunter."

The woman frowned at him. "I don't know if that's a good thing or a bad thing."

"Exactly," he said. "Honestly, I'm expecting this to be a quick visit. Check to make sure it's the same dog, make sure the hunter knows we keep track of these dogs and make sure he'll give the dog a good life, that he's healthy and well-adjusted because PTSD isn't anything for anybody to laugh about."

She stared at him. Then, as if the tumblers in her brain went *click*, she said, "But, if the dog's got PTSD, he shouldn't be out with a hunter," she exclaimed. "That would be the worst place for him."

"Which is one of the reasons I'm checking on him," he explained gently. He didn't have any clue what he was supposed to do beyond that. Maybe take the retired War Dog to one of the training complexes, like the one in Kentucky. They might have answers for Katch—or at least suggestions. Zane shrugged his shoulders irritably. "Outside of a Good Samaritan trip, I'm not sure why I'm coming to Maine."

"You're coming to Maine because you need to," she said. "Beyond that, it's up to you." And on that note she went back to her book and stayed quiet for the rest of the trip.

Zane got off the airplane, walked through the terminal and stood outside, smiling because, really, he loved his hometown. He'd always enjoyed this area. He needed to get his rental vehicle and maybe stop in at his older brother's place. That would be the one person Zane wanted to see. Although he doubted his brother would care. His dad was still around too, but that had never been an easy relationship. His father, already a difficult man, became an ugly drunk after his mother's death. The three brothers had been subjected to steady abuse while growing up.

Zane was hoping bygones could be bygones, and maybe, with any luck, his father might have eased back on the alcohol. Zane hadn't left under a cloud. In fact, he'd left for the military. But, after his younger brother Brody's death, the family dynamics had been even harder. His father had made it clear that the wrong son had died. ... As it was, Zane's life had blown up not a year later, and he'd been medically discharged himself. But at least he was still alive.

Then, when his baby brother's widow, Holly, who was also Zane's ex-girlfriend, had turned to him for comfort, things had gotten worse. He'd walked away from that real fast. Even now he couldn't understand all the ins and outs of his emotional state at that time. Except the biggest one had been guilt. He felt so damn guilty that his baby brother had died and that Zane was still alive.

Brody had been a hell of a guy—a homebody, happy to stay in this little town working at the local school, crafty with his hands, one of those all-round family-type guys. Brody had been the gym teacher and the health science teacher and an assistant coach as needed, depending on how many prospects were interested in playing football or baseball. In such a small school, there weren't many athletic students, so forming teams led to logistical problems. But Brody loved it.

Zane had understood when Holly had hooked up with Brody, after breaking up with Zane, but it had still hurt. Seeing the two of them together had just reinforced the rightness of his decision to leave for the military. And, every time he came back, it had eased a little bit more.

But the last trip home had been for his baby brother's funeral. And Holly had expected Zane to step in and to help her out, but he couldn't. It wasn't fair to drop it on Butch, but his eldest brother had been the roughneck of the family—capable, dogged and determined to handle everything in life. He was so like their father and so determined to not be their father that he'd stepped forward without a comment and had handled the funeral arrangements easily. Zane had stayed to the end, then caught the first flight back out again. His compassionate leave was up anyway, but he wouldn't have stayed and wouldn't have asked for an extension. It had just been too damn awkward. His heart hurt; his father was angry. Holly was devastated, and Zane couldn't help but think that maybe there was hope for him again with Holly.

And that had just added to the guilt. He'd raced away as fast as he could, which didn't say much for who he was.

He signed off on the airport's rental agreement for a pickup, walked out to the parking lot and hit the beeper on his key fob to find the right vehicle.

He checked his cell phone before he started the double-cab truck, found a text from his brother.

If you get in town on time, come for dinner.

He hit Dial as he pulled out onto the main road. When his brother answered, he said, "Hey, Butch. It's me, Zane. Just leaving. I'll be at your place in maybe forty minutes."

"See you then," his brother answered in his deep voice. And he hung up.

Zane tossed his phone on the seat beside him. That was so damn typical of his brother. Minimal words, minimal emotion. Unless he had a drink in his hand.

Zane sure hoped Butch hadn't followed in their father's footsteps. They'd had enough trouble with their drunken father throughout the years. Zane would not like to see that be Butch's end too.

The drive was pleasant enough. He smiled as he passed markers that brought back memories. The path to the lake they used to take every day in the summer—he could even see the small island in the middle that they used to swim out to. He drove past the corner store, then on past the only school in the area. He chuckled, remembering what it had been like going to school in a small town like this. They'd known everyone. Everyone had known each other, and every relationship had been public knowledge. It had been both great and disturbing.

By the time he pulled into his brother's driveway, he was more than ready for a chance to meet up with everyone and to sit down to have a hot meal.

His brother's driveway was long, lined with bushes and rutted, always rutted. As if his brother figured anybody without a pickup didn't belong. Zane drove carefully in the weird half-light, trying not to bounce the rental around too much.

By the time he got to the log house, the lights from within warmed his heart. He pulled up, noted his brother's new truck—a great big black F-250 diesel—and whistled. "All the bells and whistles on this one," he said out loud. His older brother, the long-haul trucker, loved the big-ass vehicles. Zane left his overnight bag and jean jacket inside his rented pickup, locked up and headed to the front step. Midway he stopped and frowned. *Maybe the secret to Butch and Sandra's marriage has been all that time apart.* Zane blew out a long exhale. *Didn't work for me and Holly.*

The door opened. There was Butch.

Zane pointed at his brother's truck. "Nice ride."

"Yep," Butch said with a shrug, motioning for his brother to come in before turning, leaving the door wide open.

And that was as much of a greeting as Zane would ever get.

Inside, Zane was not surprised to see Sandra sitting at the dining table, waiting for him. He gave her a quick hug and a kiss on the cheek. He really liked her but didn't know how she stood his brother, even for short periods of time. But, hey, that was what family was all about, trying to love them in spite of themselves, even when they weren't likeable. She bounced up to serve dinner.

"I'm sorry I delayed your dinner," Zane said. "You didn't have to wait for me."

"I wasn't going to," Butch said, "but Sandra insisted."

Zane smiled up at his sister-in-law as she gave him a great big bowl of hearty stew. "Thanks very much, Sandra."

"You're more than welcome," she said firmly. "It's really good to see you."

"Yeah, and I wonder why you're here," Butch said. "A little short on the messages, aren't you?"

"You're a fine one to talk," Zane said. "I told you that I was coming, and you gave me a very short answer yourself."

"I figured we'd have time to talk while you were here," Butch said, "unless you're not sticking around for long again."

Butch made it sound like that was a habit of Zane's. And, true enough, when Zane was on leave, he couldn't stick around very long, and he'd been in the military for a lot of years—seven before he was medically moved out. Medical discharge, they called it. He shook his head, taking his first bite of stew, then swallowing. "That's what life in the military is like."

"But you haven't been in the military for almost a year

now," Butch said. "This is the first time you've come home."

"I almost didn't come this time," Zane said quietly. He took another taste of the stew and smiled. "You're as good a cook as ever, Sandra."

She beamed at him. "Are you okay?" she asked. "We heard you were medically discharged."

"I was," he said. "Spent some time in the hospital, spent some time in rehab and, of course, then spent some time getting back to the world. Life in the military doesn't prepare you for returning to civilian life."

Her face flushed with a worried frown.

He reached across the table and patted her hand. "I'm fine now."

"Are you working?" Butch asked.

"More or less. I'm doing a job for Titanium Corp out of Santa Fe," he murmured.

No way anybody here in this corner of the woods would know Badger and his group, so they wouldn't understand that Titanium Corp was really an umbrella company for helping vets do whatever they needed to do. Zane still thought Badger was wrong when he decided that Zane needed to come to Maine. Surely he could have done something else. But, as he enjoyed the stew in front of him, he realized the trip wasn't all bad. As a matter of fact, it was pretty darn good at the moment.

"Did the job bring you home?" his brother asked abruptly.

Zane thought about his answer and realized maybe Butch would know where this dog could be. "I'm after a dog," he said.

His brother slowly lowered his fork and stared at him, disgust and contempt written all over his face.

Zane loved that his brother never failed to disappoint him.

"A dog?" Butch said in disbelief. "You came all the way across the country for a *dog*?"

"A special dog," Zane said. "A War Dog. One that, due to a series of odd circumstances, ended up with a hunter for a while but could be missing again."

"That's hardly unusual," his brother said. "Lots of hunters here have dogs. Why do you care?"

Zane looked at his brother. "Because this dog has PTSD," he said. "He was a War Dog, sent home when he couldn't handle the live action anymore."

"A bullet would be easier," his brother snapped and took another bite of stew.

"Easier?"

"Certainly cheaper," he said. "The dog is ruined. So you'll find him and put a bullet in him. It's the only answer."

"Not quite," Zane said carefully. "We don't do that to our veterans, and these dogs are veterans. They all served our military, saving as many American lives as they could. Because the dog ran into too much live action, he now can't sleep or rest, and just because he doesn't have somebody he can count on in his new life mission doesn't mean he deserves a bullet. He was lost at the airport upon arrival and never did end up with the chosen adoptive family for him. He ran away, as far as we know, but could have been on the run most of the time. The last we heard was a hunter had him and potentially doesn't any longer."

"So it's all good then," his brother said in disgust. "What a waste of time and money."

"I don't understand," Sandra said. "If he's got a home now, what's the problem?"

"Can you see the problem with a dog now paired with a hunter, when the dog has PTSD from being in the middle of too many battles?"

She winced. "Yes, that would be a problem."

"So I have a question for both of you. Do you know of any dogs that are aggressive, out-of-control, with odd behavior or just new to the area?"

"It doesn't matter. In all cases except the last one," Butch said, "they'd be taken out back and given a bullet."

And that was the end of the matter for him. Zane had figured as much, but he'd hoped his brother might have changed a little. He turned to Sandra. "What about you?"

"No," she said. "I haven't heard of anyone. But you should check with Holly."

His heart froze. "Why would I call her?" he asked, his tone harsh.

She stared at him. "She's still family."

He shrugged. "Maybe," he said. "If she hasn't remarried, that is."

"Doesn't matter if she has or not," Sandra said firmly. "She was family, and she still is family."

"Fine. Why should I contact her?"

"She's a veterinarian, remember? She might know about the dog."

He frowned and sat back. "Right. I hadn't considered that. Is she now working in her field?"

"Yes, she's a fully licensed vet," Butch said proudly. "She's done well for herself, in spite of losing our brother."

"Good for her," Zane said. He nodded to Sandra. "Good tip. Maybe I'll give her a shout and see if she knows anything." He proceeded to finish his stew.

An uncomfortable silence remained throughout the rest

of the meal. Zane checked his watch a couple times and then said, "I should probably go. Dad's expecting me."

"I doubt it," Butch said. "I haven't heard from him all day. I asked him if you had contacted him. He said yep, but that's all he said."

"In other words, nothing has changed," Zane said. He got to his feet, not looking forward to the upcoming confrontation.

"Nope, he hasn't changed a bit, except maybe he's packing in an extra bottle a week now."

Zane stared in disbelief at his brother. "How could he possibly do that and still function?"

"Nobody said he's functioning," Butch said cryptically. He nodded at the front door. "But you better be going. Otherwise Dad will probably shoot you before you get up the driveway."

On that note Zane made his way out to the rented truck and headed back to the main road. Some things never changed. His brother was barely friendly; his sister-in-law was always lovely, and his father was always scary as hell.

His father's place was just a few miles away, but, if what Butch had said was correct, Zane might need to call before he headed up the driveway. His father was a bit of a wild card. Once he got into the booze, it was hard to say what his dad's welcome would entail. Zane did not want to end up shot before he had a chance to see if Katch was here.

He parked at the head of the driveway and pulled out his phone. Before he had a chance to make a call, an SUV came down the driveway. It stopped as if to pull onto the main road, but instead the driver looked over at him. He swore softly. It was Holly, his lovely sister-in-law and ex-girlfriend.

Her face lit up. She opened the vehicle's door and ran

toward him.

He turned off his engine, hopped out and caught her as she swung into his arms, wrapping herself tightly around him. In spite of himself, he hugged her back, allowing himself just once to breathe in the scent of her hair. She always used some shampoo and conditioner that left his senses reeling.

She leaned back and beamed up at him. "I heard you were coming. I just couldn't believe it. And here you are."

"What were you doing up at Dad's?"

"Actually," she said, "I was checking to see if you were there."

He stepped back, letting his arms fall away, letting go of Holly. *Again.* "I just got in." He looked up at the house and frowned. "Butch said Dad might shoot me before I ever made it up to the house."

"Oh, Butch was just pulling one on you."

He slid her a sideways glance and then shook his head. "I don't think so. Butch isn't much of a joker."

Her hopeful expression eased slightly, and she nodded. "Okay, so your dad's had a rough couple years. Ever since Brody died."

Zane wanted to correct her and say, *Dad has had a couple rough decades. Ever since Mom died.* But he didn't. "Of course," Zane said. "I think we all went through a rough time over that."

"Your dad's looking forward to seeing you," she said, watching and waiting for his response.

Not likely.

"I'll drive up with you. It'll help break the ice."

His gaze went from the house back to her and back to the house again. "He might not shoot me flat-out that way," he said, half joking.

She hopped back into her SUV, turned it around and drove back up to the house. He followed. She hadn't changed a bit. Five foot five, and she still didn't weigh more than one hundred pounds, still had riotous curls—almost an afro, which she kept clipped back but never seemed to contain her hair completely.

He pulled up beside her. As they got out, he didn't know how he felt. Coming home was just too much all at once. He already wanted to run.

He stiffened his spine and walked to the front door.

She had it open. "Jeffrey, I met up with Zane at the bottom of the driveway."

Nothing but silence came from inside.

"Jeffrey, you there?"

"In the back," came the hollering voice.

She waited until Zane got in and shut the door behind him. It was the same old log house he'd been raised in. His mom had passed away when he was six, so Brody was four, and Butch had been only eight. Life hadn't been the same since. Their dad had been rough-and-ready and very raw around the edges. He picked up drinking not long afterward.

The boys had pretty-well raised themselves, their father even saying once, "If you live, you live. If you die, I'll bury you out back." Zane had never forgotten those words.

He followed Holly through the old house, his hands in his pockets, hating that they were already clenched. He walked inside the big living room to find his father sitting beside the fireplace, a book in his hand. Well, the addition of the book was new, but, then again, the large half-empty whiskey bottle sitting on the coffee table wasn't.

His father looked up at him and frowned. Zane frowned

right back.

HOLLY SHOULDN'T HAVE been quite so eager to see Zane, but she'd been waiting for him ever since her husband, Brody, had passed away. It was hard to explain what had happened between her and Zane before she ended up with his younger brother. She just knew she didn't want to lose that connection to Zane. Now that she was single again, she'd had more than a few thoughts and dreams that maybe they could pick up where they'd left off. But Zane had disappeared as quickly as he'd arrived for the funeral, and she'd been in shock and grieving for the first six months.

When she'd recovered, she'd dated for a while but realized she was just biding her time until Zane came home. And how unfair was that? Both to her dates and to herself. Because Zane had made a point of making sure he never did return.

She'd been in love with Zane for as long as she could remember. She hated what she'd done to them. She knew it had taken two, but she'd been the catalyst that had broken them up, and she'd compounded it by letting his younger brother sweet-talk her into a relationship. Once she'd taken that step, she knew Zane wouldn't come back to her. There was just something about going out with his brother, as if she'd crossed a line.

She had had several girlfriends who had dated multiple males in the same family without the same consequences, but Zane wasn't just anybody. And, once she'd gotten into a relationship with Brody, she'd tried hard to make the best of it because she knew Zane was gone to her. He would never be hers again. She'd then changed her attitude, her perspective, and she'd grown to love her husband.

They'd had a couple happy years, until he got sick. It had happened so damn fast. The doctors called it a staph infection, one that had run out of control. By the time she got him to the hospital to try to stop it, it had already taken over his system, and he died soon afterward.

She stared down at her hands, hating the memories that still made her insides cry. She should have forced Brody to go to the doctor earlier, but he was stubborn—so damn stubborn.

She looked up to see the two men formally greeting each other with silence and grimacing faces. There was no physical contact, not even a smile from either one. She stepped forward and said to Zane, "It's really nice to have you back for a bit."

Zane nodded, cast her a glance and then looked at his dad again.

She could see his gaze taking in the bottle at the old man's side.

Zane motioned at the closest chair. "May I sit?"

His father's frown deepened.

She rushed to fill the gap. "Of course you can. I can put on some coffee, if you'd like."

"Thank you," Zane said. "It depends if my dad's okay with that."

"Coffee would be fine," his father grumbled. "Did you stop in to see Butch?"

Zane nodded. "It was good to see Sandra and Butch. I had dinner with them."

Holly smiled at that. "Sandra's a sweetheart." Butch, well, Butch was the same as his father: taciturn, quiet, very black-and-white in many ways.

"Why are you here?" Jeffrey asked.

Holly winced at that, but it was so damn typical. She hated the stiltedness between the two of them. When growing up, the brothers hadn't gotten along with each other. None of them had gotten along with their father either. Back then it had been each man on his own—with Brody, the baby, as the dad's favorite.

In the kitchen she made a pot of coffee, and, as it dripped, she rejoined the men. Still, there wasn't a word exchanged between the two.

Zane asked her, "Have you heard of any dogs in the area being super-aggressive or very difficult? Causing concern among the locals?"

She frowned at him. "I don't recall offhand. I'd have to give that some thought. Why?"

"I'm here on behalf of the government's War Dogs program. Checking into one dog that was shipped home with PTSD, then was lost at the airport and maybe picked up a couple times by people along the way. Last reported location we have for him is in this area, maybe with a hunter. However, since the dog has PTSD, a hunter isn't the proper placement for him."

She nodded slowly. "No, it certainly wouldn't be." She sat down between the two men. "I haven't heard of one around here. I was talking to another vet though, who said he'd had a report of trouble with a dog. A man came in with a bite mark, and he was looking to hunt down the dog and kill him."

"Did he say what kind of dog it was?"

"Shepherd crossed with something, but it was bigger than usual. And I think it was male," she said, frowning. She shook her head and looked up at him. "I can call him in the morning, if you think it's important."

"Yes. I have a photo, but it's in the truck," he said with a glance back in the direction of his rented vehicle.

"You know what to do with those animals," his father snapped.

Holly winced because it was hard enough being a vet, but, in this part—the outskirts of town—where the attitude toward dogs was they'd either survive or wouldn't, that mind-set made trying to save the animals that much more difficult. The people in town were much more likely to look after their pets than those who lived out of town. The out-of-town attitude toward animals was more cavalier. Not that this was the middle of nowhere, ... though sometimes the attitude Holly came up against seemed like it. Jeffrey was a loner. Butch was headed in the same direction. If not for Sandra, he probably would be as isolated as Jeffrey was. She didn't think Zane was like that. As she looked at him now, she realized he'd been through something he hadn't shared with the rest of them. "You're no longer military, so why are you doing this for the War Dogs division?"

"As a favor for friends and a company I work for."

"At least you're working," his father snapped. He turned his gaze back to the fireplace.

"Yes, I am working," Zane said.

"What are you doing?" Holly asked hopefully.

She wished she'd met him somewhere else, somewhere they could sit down and actually be friendly, but attention to Zane would likely be construed as inappropriate by his father. Jeffrey was a lot of things, but he'd loved Brody something fierce—unfortunately much more than he had ever loved his other two sons. But then Brody had been the baby of the family. Maybe that was to be expected.

"I'm doing this job as a favor for a commander. He needed somebody to find a dozen missing War Dogs, to see if they were doing okay. We raised these animals to serve our military, our country. They were well-trained and, in some cases, trained to be killers," Zane admitted. "We don't want them loose, running around hurting people, but neither do we want the dogs to be hurt. We've tracked down two already. This is the third."

"And were the dogs okay? Were they hurting people?"

"We had different men on the individual cases. In the first case, the dog ended up in a drug-manufacturing complex, used as a watchdog. They were trying to train him to kill on command. Ethan, who was assigned that case, now has up to five dogs he's working with so far," Zane said with a half smile. "In the second case, Pierce went to Pete's place, as the owner and handler, but Pete was badly injured and medically discharged along with his K9. Once there, Pierce found out the dog had been abused and mistreated by the locals who were trying to use it for hunting. The dog had run off, but Pierce got the dog back together with Pete, and Pierce got Pete back home too. So I'd say that's a good ending to the story right there."

"And what about this one?" Holly asked, frowning. "If he's dangerous, he'll likely be put down."

"Maybe he's dangerous, and maybe he's not," Zane said. "We usually find it's people who are more dangerous to the dogs."

"That's the way it should be," his father growled. "Dogs are working animals. If they can't work, they don't get fed."

"Says you," Zane said calmly. He sipped his coffee and looked at it, smiling. "Thanks for the coffee, Holly."

Holly stared at the cup in her hand, surprised she'd already poured two cups and brought them back so fast that she hadn't even realized what she was doing. "Jeffrey, do you want a cup?"

"Not now." He shook his head, staring into the fire.

She turned toward Zane. "Where are you staying?"

He gave a flat stare directed at his father. "I was hoping I could grab my bed for the night. If this isn't a welcome location, then I'll find a place tomorrow."

"It's just your dad here, so I'm sure that's not a problem," she said encouragingly. "Jeffrey, is it okay?" She'd learned the best way to deal with these Carmichael men was to ask a direct question, one where they either had to give her a yes or no answer. Too often she didn't like the answer, but at least they'd given one.

"Be on your way in the morning," he said.

She caught the glimmer of a smile on Zane's face.

"Will do," he said.

He portrayed that casual I-don't-give-a-shit attitude. But she knew he did care.

"If you need a place to stay while you're around," she said, "I'm in town. I've got lots of room, so don't get a hotel room when you could be among friends."

"Not sure where I'll end up," he said quietly. "But thank you for the kind offer."

She realized his brother probably hadn't offered either. She sighed and sagged back in the chair. "Not everybody is as unfriendly as you may think."

"Are you sure?" he asked as he turned to look at his father. "Are you still working?"

"Haven't for a long time," he said.

She filled in for them again. "He retired from the post

office just after Brody passed away." She gazed back at Zane's flat stare. How was it he didn't know this? But then again, look at the two of them now. It wasn't as if they even communicated when they were in the same room. She glanced at her watch. "I've got to go. It's late already."

Zane looked down and nodded. "It's almost nine o'clock." He frowned. "Are you okay to drive back alone?"

She laughed. "I've been driving this road a long time," she said.

"Or you could live here now and not make the night drive," Jeffrey said.

She reached out and patted his arm. "Thank you. I know, but I need to be in town for my job." She took her cup back into the kitchen. When she came out to the entranceway, Zane waited for her.

They stepped out in the front yard, and he closed the door behind him. "What's he living on?" Zane asked abruptly. "I can't imagine any retirement check would be big enough to cover his liquor bill much less anything else."

She shrugged. "I have no clue. But there's food in the cupboards, and he's got power, and there's gas in his tank because I see him driving around every once in a while. So he's getting by somehow."

Zane nodded, crossed his arms over his chest and stared out in the night. "Some things never change."

"And yet, some things do," she said with a sudden tiredness. "Anyway, if you need a place to stay, as I told you, you're welcome to my guest room." She opened her purse and pulled out a business card. "That's my work number, but, if you call, let the girls know who you are, and I'll give you a shout back. Otherwise, I hope you have a good stay." She bravely turned and walked toward her vehicle.

"How much do you have to do with him?"

She looked back at Zane. "Probably not enough," she said. "Your father is all alone. I stayed with him for a while after we lost Brody, but then it was time to get my life together again. I don't think he appreciated that I moved out, but it was what I needed to do."

Zane shoved his hands in his jeans pockets and rocked on his heels, nodding. "It makes sense."

"Does it? How does any of this make any sense at all?" she cried out, raising both hands in frustration. Seeing yet another flat stare of his, this time directed at her, she hopped into her SUV and drove away.

How the hell had she loved two men from the same damn family? And a family full of obstinate and difficult men?

CHAPTER 2

THE NEXT MORNING Holly headed to work after a really bad night. She kept waking up with pictures of Brody dying again in her dreams, yet his face was superimposed with images of Zane's face. They'd always been confused in her head. She'd understood it was her own fault, but that didn't change anything.

"Wow, you look like you need coffee," Mittle said as Holly came through the glass double doors at the front of the office.

Groaning, Holly nodded. "You're so right. Have you got any made?"

"Coming up," her assistant said. "As a matter of fact, it's almost done."

"Great," Holly said. "I didn't get much sleep last night."

"Still got bad dreams?"

"Yeah, they were much worse last night though." She walked through to the back, smiling to see Katlyn, her vet assistant, checking over Maxie, a big tomcat. They'd put stitches in his ear and patched up a gash along his back—his tomfoolery days were now over. "How is our guest?" she asked.

"He's feisty but looking for attention."

"Maybe contact Selena at the shelter and see if she has room for him. I hate to release him back out in the wild. Or at least maybe find a farmer or a rancher where he can be a barn cat."

"I love that you treat a lot of our local feral animals for free. You name them, for God's sake. You've got a good heart, Holly. But we're up against an incessant problem with cats, aren't we?"

"We are often. The harsh winters take our numbers down, but, if we could at least catch, fix and release, it would help."

"We could do that with this one, but you said you didn't want to."

"Because I'd rather catch, fix and release into a new home for these guys," Holly said, walking through to her office. "What kind of a day do we have scheduled?"

"It's office hours all day," Mittle said, "and we're booked up."

Holly nodded, headed for her desk, sitting down, ready to cry. She didn't know why she was so emotional, weepy. It would never do though. Her staff only ever saw her with a bright, cheerful attitude, not this one—where all she wanted to do was go home, curl up in bed and forget the world had come and gone. She hated to think Brody was her last chance at love and life, but it'd seemed like it for so long, until she saw Zane again. Then she realized everything inside of her wanted Zane to come back into her life again.

She checked her calendar, saw it really was a full day, opened her email and ran through that until she heard the initial buzzer. She got up, headed into the first treatment room to find it empty. She walked through to the front office. "Did I mistake that buzz for a patient?"

"Well, maybe a patient," Mittle said, "and maybe not." She pointed to a man in the center of the room. "He came in looking for you."

She looked up and smiled. "Zane. I wasn't expecting you so early."

He gave her a crooked grin. "Should have been here earlier and then we could have gone for breakfast."

"She doesn't have a patient for at least an hour," Mittle said to Zane. Then she turned to Holly. "Your first appointment is canceled."

"It should be more than one that canceled for me to have an hour free," Holly said jokingly.

"So how about forty-five minutes?" Mittle replied.

Holly looked over at Zane. "We can step into the diner next door, if you want."

He nodded. "Sounds good."

Instead of waiting for her, he left and waited on the front step.

"Wow, that's a bit of an untamed animal in his own right," Mittle said with an odd breath. "He looks damn familiar though. Who the hell is he?"

Holly laughed. "That's Zane. Zane Carmichael."

"Shit, really? Brody's brother?"

"And Butch's brother and Jeffrey's middle son."

"There's definitely a family resemblance," Mittle said. "But, wow, this one looks like, I don't know, there's just something almost extremely wild about him."

"Maybe Sandra thought the same thing when she hooked up with Butch," Holly said. "Zane's back looking for a dog, a War Dog last seen in this area. Could be dangerous to humans, but Zane wants to ensure the dog has a good life."

"You were talking to Reggie about a dog yesterday. That might have been the one Zane was talking about."

"Oh, I forgot about that." Holly frowned. "Write down Reggie's contact info and address for me, will you? So I can give it to Zane."

Mittle opened up the files, checked for Reggie's info and wrote it down for Holly. "Enjoy your breakfast," she said. She leaned closer. "And remember. It's been two years. Nobody would blame you if you wanted to do the hubba-hubba with this guy."

Holly snorted at that and walked out. Good thing nobody really understood that she had already done the hubba-hubba with this guy, and it had been the best damn hubba-hubba she'd ever had.

ZANE WAITED UNTIL she stepped up beside him. "Ready?"

She nodded. "You didn't have to wait outside."

"I'm an outdoor man," he said and led the way to the coffee shop. "Besides, I don't want your staff to get the wrong idea."

"What idea would that be?" she asked drily. "I haven't seen you since the funeral. That's too long to make anybody think anything."

"Probably better that way," he said.

"How do you figure?" she asked.

He could hear the curiosity in her voice. He shrugged, didn't answer.

They walked into the café, sat down and ordered coffee. She handed over the vet's name and number. "This is the guy I mentioned last night, telling me about a dangerous dog in his area."

"Thanks. I'll give him a call as soon as we're done here."

"What will you do when you find the dog?"

"I'm not sure," he said. "I guess it depends on the circumstances."

"You really feel for him, don't you?"

He folded the piece of paper and put it in his wallet while she watched. He nodded. "Yes, I do. I have PTSD myself. The dog and I are kindred spirits. Although I have some skill with animals, I wasn't part of the military's K9 unit. And I don't know how this dog will do in the real world."

"Kind of like you too, huh?" She hesitated, then added, "Was your PTSD that bad?"

He shot her a shuttered look, then a clipped nod. "My case could be much worse though, so I try not to focus on the negatives."

"Meaning, you don't want to talk about it," she said.

He slid her a look. "Exactly."

"Did you see your father at all last night again? Did you guys talk?"

"*Humph*," Zane snorted. "I went back inside, and he was gone. I went up to bed, got up this morning but saw no sign of him. He'd already left the house. I don't know where he went because I'd think it was too early for a liquor store to be open. I just hopped into my truck and came here. Like he said, it was okay for me to stay the one night, but I'm not welcome back."

"That is a shame," she said quietly. "I know you guys didn't always get along, but right now you'd think the loss of Brody would pull you together, not push you further apart."

"I think he figures, as long as he has Butch and you close by, he doesn't need me."

He couldn't even decide for himself if that hurt or not.

He'd become accustomed to it a long time ago. The younger Zane would have been hurt, but the older one—who'd seen his father so set in his ways, and Butch just following right along behind him—wasn't sure he wanted anything to do with either of them. They were family, at least by blood, but, if a family didn't give a shit, why should he?

"Brody got along with him," she said.

"Hell yeah, because Dad loved Brody. Dad probably only loved two people in his whole life. Our mother and Brody. Of course it was Dad's version of love."

"After Brody's death, I think your father went to pieces. I stayed in the house as long as I could, more for his sake than mine, but it was like a restraint wrapped around me. As if he didn't expect me to move on with my life."

"You weren't supposed to," Zane said. "God knows Dad never did."

"Right."

The waitress walked over and handed them menus.

Holly looked up, smiled and said, "Hi, Sally. I'll have the special, please."

Zane returned his menu and said, "I'll have the same thing."

The waitress noted their orders and disappeared.

Zane looked at Holly and asked, "What about you? Have you picked up your life and moved on?"

"Only as far as moving back and being independent, working at my clinic," she said. "I have two other vets I work with, so it's a shared process, but at least I'm doing what I was meant to do."

"I didn't mean to upset you. I guess I don't quite know how to get over the blocks of the past."

"Coming home is a good way to start," she said.

"And yet, look what happens when I do come home," he said.

"I haven't really started dating again," she said abruptly. "Tried a few casual coffee dates, but that's all."

He studied her features for a long moment. "When you do, I'm sure you won't lack for suitors."

"And what does that mean?" she asked, her voice edgy.

He raised his head and studied her more clearly. "Nothing. Just that you're an attractive young woman, and I'm sure you won't have any trouble finding a new partner in life."

"Do you think that's what I want, a new partner in my life?"

He frowned at her. "This is starting to sound like we're arguing. I didn't intend that. I was trying to tell you that you're attractive, and I'm sure lots of men would like to go out with you."

He didn't understand the fathomless look in her eyes. It looked like she wanted to say something. He was glad she didn't because he wasn't sure he was up for any melodramatic conversations. They had a history, but the history needed to be kept in the background. He still couldn't reconcile the fact that she'd been his kid brother's wife. It might be his issue, but, because it involved her, it was still her issue to deal with too.

"I've been asked," she said slowly, "but I keep holding whoever it is up to the same yardstick that I held you and your brother up to."

"Nobody can measure up to Brody. He was your choice, so he'll be the best in your mind. You have to accept either there's another best choice or there'll be somebody less than Brody but who will still make you happy."

She stared at him in surprise. "Is that why you think I married Brody?"

He frowned at her. "I hope so, for Brody's sake."

At that, she fell silent.

"I don't understand what this conversation is about," he said slowly. "Are you saying Brody wasn't your best choice? He wasn't the man you loved?"

"I married him because I loved him," she said quietly. "And because I no longer had a relationship with you."

He stared at her. "Of course you didn't. We broke up." He took a deep breath, adding, "And then you went out with my brother."

"I went out with your brother because it was as close as I could get to you," she admitted slowly. "I hate to admit it, but that was my original reason for going out with him. I think the real reason he wanted to go out with me was because I was *your* girlfriend. As if some jealousy was there, or he wanted something you had. I don't know." She waved her hand as if to brush it away. "Over time I did love him, and we were happy when we were married."

"Good," he said. "I wouldn't want it any other way."

She frowned at him. "This is a silly conversation."

"Agreed," he snapped, feeling uncertain and irritated, not knowing why. "So let's find something else to talk about."

"Like what?" she asked. "All there ever was between us was *us*. One of the reasons we couldn't stay together was we never could talk. You never would share your feelings or let me know what you were thinking."

"Well, that hasn't changed," he said. "I still don't share very much. After my accident, it got worse. I spent a lot of time in the hospital, a lot of time in rehab. I was alone then, and I'm still alone now."

"And, like you just suggested to me," she said, "you don't have to be. I'm sure any number of women want to spend time with you."

"Maybe," he said, "but that doesn't mean I want to spend time with them."

"What is it you're looking for?"

He stared out the window, knowing he couldn't tell her. "What I want is what I can't have."

"Maybe you should be honest for once and tell me what it is you really want."

He looked at her but again shuttered his gaze. Just then the waitress arrived, saving him from giving Holly an answer, even an evasive one.

He looked down at the large breakfast in front of him and smiled. "Well, this was worth coming into town early for. I wasn't going to get any breakfast at home."

"You should have stayed with me then," Holly said with a bit of snap to her voice. "I would have at least fed you."

CHAPTER 3

A S THEY WALKED out of the diner, her phone rang. She checked it to see the same Caller ID information she'd given to Zane earlier. "Hey, Reggie. How are you doing?"

"I'm okay. Just short on a couple medications and wondered what your supply is like?"

"I'm walking back to the clinic now. I can take a look. Tell me what you need," she said, nodding a couple times. "While I have you, a man I know is looking for a dog, a War Dog, last seen in this area. He's tracking him down to make sure he's okay. So he's asking questions about any aggressive dogs or untamed dogs, dogs causing problems. You know what I mean?" she added with a sidelong look at Zane.

He raised an eyebrow at her but waited patiently at her side.

"I've got one in right now," Reggie said. "He's in the back pen, but I'll have to restrain him before I can deal with him."

"What happened to him?"

"Honestly it looks like somebody tried to shoot him and did a shitty job."

"Male, female, shepherd, what?"

"Very dark-colored shepherd crossed with something. He's got the caramel-colored eyebrows, but everything else appears to be black. Decent size so likely mixed with something bigger."

"Does he have a name tag, tattoo, anything like that?"

"No idea. I haven't been able to check. He's next on my list. But he's not taking any of our medication the easy way, so I'll have to use a dart gun on him. I can't get close enough to use a syringe."

"How did you get him into the pen in the first place?" she asked curiously, holding the phone out so Zane could hear.

"He was dropped off barely conscious. Found on the side of the road apparently. We moved him into the yard, and he came awake, fighting and trying to bolt. So he's functioning and mobile, but he's definitely pissed off. Now I have to find a way to get close enough to him to knock him out."

"May I come over and take a look?" Zane asked, leaning into the phone.

"Sure. If you can control this animal, all the better. Otherwise I'm not sure what'll happen to him."

"Was a complaint registered against him?"

"No, but it looks awfully similar to the one that we've got a complaint about from several homeowners."

"And, of course, that's a death sentence right there," she said, her voice quiet. They both did as many charity cases as they could afford and the community helped out with various fund-raising but if it wasn't kept up, the money dried up very quickly. There was always more animals in need than they could handle.

"I know. I don't know what happened to the dog. His coat is pretty thick and rough. Something's definitely not quite right about it. I'll have to take a better look when I can get him on my table."

"If you don't mind Zane coming over, he can deliver the drugs too," Holly said as she walked into the vet clinic. "I think I have what you need."

"Perfect. If you can invoice me for it, I'd appreciate it. I've got surgery scheduled this afternoon, and our shipment was supposed to arrive this morning but didn't. At least not yet."

"It will probably come tomorrow."

"I wouldn't be surprised," he said, fatigue in his voice. "I don't know about you, but our schedule here is nuts."

"Yep, same here. I'm booked up all day, every day. It's both good and bad," she said with a light laugh.

"Exactly," he said. "But, right about now, it'd be awfully nice if I were dealing with trimming toenails and checking infected ears versus dealing with vicious dogs that have been shot."

"Have you had more than one?" Zane asked.

"Third one this week," he said. "The first one I couldn't do anything but put it out of its misery. It was almost dead anyway. The second one was shot in the hindquarters. Pretty well glanced off and opened up a nasty wound in the flank. I'm not sure who's against dogs in this county, but somebody sure as hell is."

"You think it's the same person?" she asked in surprise.

"We usually find that it is, don't we?" he stated. "We often get a run of similar injuries, like car accidents, where they tend to cluster together. But these three shootings, I don't know. I highly suspect it's somebody who doesn't want anything canine close to him."

"Were these dogs pets?"

"The first one was a family pet, but it had gotten out and was running across the field. The owner saw him go down. He never did see the shooter."

"The second one?"

"The owner came home and found the dog on the front step. He was still alive, still is now," he said, "but his back legs are pretty torn up. On top of that, there's no real way of knowing who did this to him."

"Is the bullet still in the dog?" Zane asked.

"No," he said. "The first one has already been cremated, and honestly I didn't look. I wasn't too interested in pulling the bullet out. The dog was dead, and the owners didn't want to cause a fuss, which I also thought was kind of weird."

"And what about this one? Any bullet?"

"Again I'll let you know if and when I can get him on my table," Reggie said, his tone humorous. "He's not too willing to let me take a look."

"As soon as we get the medication packed up here," Zane said into the phone, "I'll leave. I should be at your place in what, fifteen minutes?" He looked over at Holly.

Holly nodded.

"Appreciated. See you when you get here then." Reggie hung up.

Holly turned to Mittle and said, "Let's see what we've got for stock. As soon as I hand this over, we need to reorder."

She left Zane sitting in the waiting room as she went into the back and unlocked the medication cabinet. She easily had enough for Reggie, so she pulled out what he needed, marked it down, told Mittle to invoice him, put it in a bag and walked out, handing it to Zane.

"This is what he needs," she said. "His clinic is not very far from here. It's a pretty straight shot." She gave him the directions, and he nodded with almost a clipped movement that showed some restraint. She could see the tension vibrating inside him. "Are you tense because you think this might be the War Dog, and it's hurt? Or because of something else?"

He shot her a look and said, "Anytime shooting is involved, I'm not a happy camper. But anytime someone's shooting animals, I'm definitely not a happy camper. When it's dogs for no particular reason, especially if they were with their owner in their own yard, I'm even angrier," he snapped. "And you can bet I'll get to the bottom of it."

"It's not your job," she warned. "We have law enforcement here."

"That's nice," he said. "You'll have to call them then, but you can bet this dog doesn't have anybody who cares one way or another."

"You don't know that though," she urged. "Take it easy and don't go in there with preconceived ideas."

Once again came that clipped nod, and he turned, headed to the front door.

"Wait? Are you coming back this afternoon?"

He stopped briefly at the door, thought about it, then shrugged. "No clue. Depends on the dog."

She stood with her hands on her hips, waiting as he drove away, wondering what the hell had just happened. As always Zane was a bit of a storm, but, right now, he was almost a cyclone. He blew into her life and was about to blow out again. She wanted to remain unscathed, but a part of her needed to touch that energy again to see if she could keep it tethered to her this time.

No doubt he was more injured now than he'd ever been. These injuries were more psychological than physical. He'd always been a force hard to contend with. Now something was broken. No, not quite broken, she mused, as she stared blindly out the window. So maybe bruised, as if still injured where it wasn't visible. Giving her head a shake, she returned to her office and called back, "I presume the day's about to begin?"

"Yep, you already got somebody in Treatment Room 1," Mittle said. "Better get at it before we're backed up."

With a heavy sigh Holly headed off to her first patient. All she could hope was that Zane found what he needed, in more ways than one.

ZANE PULLED INTO Reggie's vet clinic, hopped out, locked his truck and walked up to the front doors. When he introduced himself and handed over the medications, the nurse's face beheld a big smile. She disappeared and came back with an older man, his wispy hair forming a ring around an otherwise bald top.

Reggie reached out a hand and said, "Nice to meet you, Zane. Thanks for the delivery."

"Not a problem," Zane said quietly. "Where's the dog?"

"Come this way."

Reggie led Zane through a long hallway to the surgery rooms where cages held various animals. And then he stepped through a glass door to a grassy area in back. On the side was a dog pen.

"He's in here," Reggie said. He walked alongside the large pen and stopped, looked from one end to the other end, and then frowned. "Or rather he was here," he snapped. He raced back inside, calling out, "Did anybody let that dog out of the fenced pen?"

Zane could hear *no* from various people being called back. He walked from one side of the grassy area to the other and saw the fence was only four feet high. Any decent shepherd could jump that in a heartbeat. It did say something to the dog's mobility, but, as Zane's sharp gaze caught tufts of fur at the far end of the fence, Zane knew the dog's mobility was definitely affected.

As soon as Reggie came out again, Zane said, "Do you mind if I go in? It looks like fur and blood are over there."

Reggie opened the gate, and they both walked in.

"So the dog is mobile, and he made this jump, but he left chunks of him behind," Zane noted. "Was he wounded along the rear right leg?"

"He was, indeed, but also along the spine. Maybe the dog was already jumping in the air when he took the bullet. I don't know. But he was hit here." He motioned with his hand to his own flank, stretching out to his back. "On the other hand, that shot could have been going the opposite direction, from the top of the spine down the flank."

"That's possible too," Zane said. He looked at a second gate, one he presumed led into a treatment room.

"Now he's gone," Reggie said. "Part of me is delighted, and another part of me is worried as hell."

"I'll follow him," Zane said. "See if I can track him down."

"I'm not sure this one is the dog you're looking for," the vet said. "Although the dog was big, the shoulders were smaller, leaner, and the hips were a little narrower. It's quite possible it was just a larger-size female."

"Won't know until I check," Zane said. "I'm after one from the War Dogs program. And he's had quite a hard time since he was medically discharged with PTSD."

"Wow," the vet said. "I know that happens to dogs all the time, but very few people consider it a condition for animals."

"It's definitely a condition for this one, so any loud noises, bullets, guns, that type of thing, will panic him even more and make him hard to deal with. But, when you said there was almost something wrong with him mentally, I would think he was probably still in shock, disoriented and dealing with his own nightmares."

"I'm so sorry to hear that," Reggie said quietly. "If I'd known, I would have tried to check him out earlier." He looked around and raised both hands in frustration. "But the business these days is seriously bad. I'm not sure what's going on, but I need another pair of hands in here," he said. "I can't keep up."

"It's hard to expect anybody to keep up with this pace," Zane said. "The vet business has grown because the local population has grown, bringing in more animals. I used to live in this area, and it's really incredibly sprawled out now, compared to what it was."

"And we have a lot more vet offices opening up. It's just not enough," he said. "It's never enough."

Without saying anything else, Zane hopped over the fence exactly at the spot where the dog had jumped and followed the tracks into a large stretch of field out behind the dog run. The area was flat, heading toward some trees. For the dog, that would have been an unmistakable lure to get away from people who'd obviously hurt him, to get away from noises obviously bothering him and to head out to the far corners as fast as he could go.

Zane picked up a blood trail, frowning as the amount of

seepage made the dog's trail obvious to follow. Both good and bad in this situation, because there were other predators than just the man who'd shot him.

Zane ran toward the tree line, hoping to find the dog unconscious somewhere between where he stood and in the trees. But it wasn't to be. Once Zane was in the tree line, it was much harder to see the blood. He stopped in the shadows, crouched, looking to pick up the trail. It took him ten minutes to find it, off about ten feet to the right, and then the dog had taken a hard left, going around trees and in a completely different direction.

Zane didn't know what had spooked him, but he was off and running again. He couldn't run anywhere near as fast as he had before, yet tracking was always a lot slower. Zane kept at it, doggedly following the blood trail, even though now it fell on dirt, soaking into the ground. With the shadows playing games with his eyesight, it took much longer to get through the woods to the other side.

There he found more green grass, more blood trails, and what looked like hills up ahead. He didn't remember this area from his childhood, which was too bad because he didn't know of any particular place where Katch would have gone to ground.

Zane followed the blood for the next half hour, wondering how badly injured the animal could be if he was still going at the pace he was moving. But these War Dogs were well-trained, and, when fear was involved, they could keep going for hours.

A creek was up ahead. Zane stopped, studied it, seeing paw prints heading into the water and coming out on the other side. Crossing the creek, he stopped, leaned against a tree and surveyed the meadow in front of him. A crackle of a branch to his right had him studying the trees closer.

He watched a man, rifle in his hand, up and ready to shoot. He could see nothing in front of the man, even out a good fifty meters. He called over to him, "Hey, don't shoot."

The man didn't appear to notice. Or he was deliberately ignoring Zane. He changed direction and headed toward the shooter. He was about twenty feet from the shooter when the man suddenly heard him and raised his sights to study him.

Zane called out, "Don't shoot that dog please."

But instead of lowering the weapon, the shooter trained it on Zane.

"Shit," Zane whispered. He stopped in his tracks, held up his hands to show he wasn't armed. "Is this what you do, hunt and shoot dogs?"

The hunter took several cautious steps backward. Good. Zane was hoping he'd turn tail and run, like the coward he was. When he came up against the first tree, the hunter stopped, kept his rifle trained on Zane, and then ducked behind the tree and disappeared into the shadows.

Zane was caught between wanting to run after the shooter and staying with the dog. But he knew the dog was injured already. Taking note of the direction the shooter had disappeared, Zane raced in the direction the shooter had been targeting. Sure enough, lying on his side was a black shepherd-cross dog. Zane approached cautiously, as the dog was still awake, a growl coming from deep in his throat.

Zane crouched and crept along until he was within six feet of the dog. He whispered, "Take it easy, Katch." He presumed it was the right dog from the photos. Even his mannerisms fit that of a War Dog. "Take it easy, boy."

His growls didn't stop though. Zane closed his eyes and willed loving energy toward Katch. Zane had always had a way with animals, but it was important they understood and received the kind of reception he wanted to give them. And it wasn't easy when animals were already injured and terrified and abused by men.

He sat at Katch's side, just talking to him calmly, trying desperately to let him know that Zane wasn't a threat. But how would Katch understand that when the last man who'd followed him back here was a big threat to Katch?

The dog lay here, breathing heavily. Zane studied his injuries and found blood on his chest and flank, running down his leg. "Well, Katch, you're big, and you're heavy, and you'll be a hard load to get back to the clinic. Especially if you don't go willingly."

He shuffled a little closer. Katch growled again, staring at him. Zane could see the whites of his eyes, and his panic already started. Katch struggled to rise, then gave a whimper and fell back on his shoulder.

Zane waited, checking to see if the animal would open his eyes again or move. Zane shuffled forward yet again, realizing Katch had lost consciousness with the pain of his injuries.

Knowing Zane would cause Katch more injuries and pain if moved, but, not really having much choice, Zane checked out the dog's wounds while he was out cold. Zane saw the bullet was still in his flank, and the dog had an open wound showing the white of a rib. The dog was easily 140 pounds, if not 180.

With great difficulty, he got his arms underneath the dog, positioned for a fireman's carry, and, using his legs, Zane slowly rose. The biggest problem would be if the dog woke up again.

Focusing, blanking out the pain caused by Katch's

weight, Zane walked steadily back the way he'd come. He had no way to phone the vet to let him know to watch for him. But, as he came through the tree line to the meadow and over to the field, he could see the vet standing in the pen, looking in his direction.

Zane let out a whistle. The vet lifted a hand, bolted indoors, out of sight. Zane certainly hoped Reggie was bringing an anesthetic to keep the dog knocked out.

As soon as Zane managed to get Katch to the clinic, Zane still had to walk around to the side, carrying the dead weight of an unconscious Katch, and then in through double doors that Reggie opened for him, while pushing a gurney.

"Lay him on this," he murmured.

Relieved to have the weight off his shoulders, he gently laid the big animal on top of the gurney. "He's unconscious. I don't know how badly injured he is, other than what you initially saw. I stopped a hunter from shooting him. He took off into the woods."

"Did you recognize him?" Reggie asked.

"No, I didn't," he said, "but then I don't know anybody around here. What I do know is, when I told him to stop, he turned that rifle on me. He then backed out and took off, but I definitely got the impression he wouldn't have cared less if he shot me or not, except for the fact we were too close to civilization, and he probably would have been caught."

Reggie shook his head. "What the hell has the world come to?" He pushed the gurney inside. "Now that the dog's out cold, I'll run through some tests and see what we've got."

"You need a hand? He's a lot to move around."

"We're set up for him," he said. "If you want to take a seat in the front room, I'll see what I can find out."

And that was as good as it would get. Zane sat down and

waited. He should have taken some photos to compare it to the pictures in his truck. Thinking about that, he walked out to his pickup and found the folder. Just then he got a message from Badger, asking for an update.

Instead of texting, Zane called and said, "I may have found him. I think I have at least. I'll get the vet to check for a chip and tattoo when he's done with the initial checkup."

"Wow, that's fast work," Badger said. "Is he okay?"

"No. I've just brought him back after a hunter tried to shoot him. Again. Katch has already got one bullet burn up the side of the shoulder and a bullet in the flank. A nasty side injury as well. He was at the vet's earlier today but bolted. I'm not sure what's going on or who's been shooting him, but somebody's a shitty shot, and they should learn to put an animal out of its misery, if that was the case. I'm not sure it was though. For all I know, somebody was just tormenting Katch."

"Bastards," Badger said with heat. "It's a tough-enough world out there as it is, but to have an animal that's done so much for our country to come home and to be treated like that ..."

"I know," Zane said. "I'm sitting in the vet's office right now, while he runs through a bunch of tests. Not exactly sure what else could be wrong until Reggie comes back out."

"Good enough," Badger said. "Make sure you let me know as soon as you hear something." He hesitated, then asked, "Is Maine as bad as you thought it would be?"

"Yes," Zane said in no uncertain terms. "So far, it's worse." And he hung up.

He didn't want to let Badger off the hook. He hadn't forced Zane to come, but Badger had certainly nudged Zane. Of course Badger didn't know what Zane was up against, but Zane did, and he didn't really want to come. But then, if that was true, why had he allowed Badger to push him? It was good to see Butch and to see he was fine. To see Sandra and he were good together. Of course their father hadn't changed a bit, except to become more of a drunk than he was before.

It was bound to be depressing to be around Holly. He had enjoyed breakfast with her, enjoyed being around her. He had been quieter than usual because he was still dealing with his reaction to being close to her. His feelings were still there, and that bothered him. One should be able to walk away from those feelings, like one walked away from the person who caused those feelings. Only it wasn't that simple.

Apparently she had a greater tug on his heart than he had thought. Their conversation this morning had been … interesting. He was glad for his brother's sake that she hadn't gone into a marriage still caring about one man while pretending to love another. His brother deserved more than that.

At the same time, it was hard for him to realize Holly and his brother had had a good marriage. Zane admitted a part of him wanted her to have been very unhappy, desperately waiting for Zane to come back. But they'd broken off because of a lot of problems. And she'd moved on.

He had too, in some ways, but hadn't found anybody else to love, like she had. He wasn't jealous; he was grateful she had a good life. Losing his brother had been hard on everybody. And it was such a stupid death. Not that there was any good death. But a staph infection brought on from a simple wound? Not fair.

He studied the folder in front of him but barely saw the pages. From the picture, the single shitty black-and-white photo he had, it looked like the male he had found. All black, and it was a shepherd–Belgian Malinois cross. Another common breed used in War Dogs.

He closed the folder, tucked it back into his briefcase and left it in his truck.

Back inside Reggie's clinic, Zane poured himself a coffee and stood in front of the window.

Finally the receptionist called to him, "The doctor will see you now."

He turned to look at her. "Where?"

"He said you can go back to the surgery room." She pointed at the door he'd been through before.

In the surgery room he saw the shepherd being moved to a large cage and winced. "He's not going to like that."

"We don't have a choice," Reggie said. "When he comes to, he won't be friendly. I've got an IV drip in him, so, if I need to, I can knock him out again."

"How bad is he?"

"A couple cracked ribs, a nasty slice on one. He needed eighty stitches," Reggie admitted. "The back hip was dislocated, and he'd lost a lot of blood. Looks like he might have been beaten, according to some of his wounds. His body was pretty badly bruised."

"Did you happen to find a tattoo and a chip?"

Reggie nodded. "Give me a second. I'll grab his file. We wrote it down." He walked away, leaving Zane to crouch beside the dog.

Zane reached out a hand within the open cage and gently stroked the dog's forehead. He was waiting for the tattoo number to confirm it, but, in his heart, he knew this was Katch. How sad he didn't appear to be having the time of his life playing catch.

When Reggie came back, he read off a number, and Zane sighed. "Yep, this is him."

"Now what?" Reggie said.

"Do you know if anybody owns him?"

Reggie shook his head. "No. I'm not sure what to do with him once we get him fixed up."

"You don't do anything," Zane said, standing up. "Now he's my responsibility. And send me his bill." He gently closed the cage. "Let me know when he wakes up and how he's doing. I'll come back tomorrow morning to spend some time with him. When you think he's free to go, I'll take him back with me."

"Back to New Mexico?" Reggie asked in fascination. "Won't be ready to fly for a bit. I'm not even sure the airlines will take him when he's as injured as he is."

Zane laughed. "No, not back there. I'm not sure where we're going yet. I'll let you know." He shook Reggie's hand and in a sincere voice said, "Thank you very much for looking after him." And he walked out.

CHAPTER 4

HOLLY WONDERED IF she would see Zane again. No matter how she agonized each time he left—leaving *her*, in her mind—and no matter how resolute her determination to not let him into her heart again, here she was doing it again. She finished a heavy day's work and sat in her office for a few minutes after the last patient had left. Normally she was in no rush to leave, taking time to make sure everything was done, but today she wanted to get out to see where Zane had ended up—hopefully make plans for dinner with him and have him back at her place. She felt compelled to get every minute of his visit that she could. She knew he would just fly away again and leave her empty and cold like he had every other time before.

She'd had a hard time when he went into the military. She understood it was his choice, but, at the same time, it seemed like he didn't care how she felt about it. Maybe that was the way of the world. She considered now, had he been against her going to vet school, if she would have still gone. Of course she would have. As an older adult, she could understand why he'd felt the need to go to into the military but back then? … No.

She stood from her desk, grabbed the last of her files and carried them to the reception area, dropping them on Mittle's desk. "Hell, that was one long-ass afternoon."

"Busy," Mittle agreed. "The days are getting like that more and more often."

"They are," Holly said, rotating her neck, then rubbing her temples. "Has everybody been picked up?"

"We're waiting on one woman who's coming in from work to get her kitty."

"So none being left overnight? That's good then. I don't have to come back or stay here."

"No, it looks like you should be free to go. Of course it wasn't a surgery day, so that makes it easier too."

"True enough," Holly said. She walked back through the surgical room, her keen eye checking to make sure everything was in order. Stock had arrived today, so that should have been dealt with. But Mittle was right. When it wasn't a surgery day, Holly had time for dealing with other elements of her job. Two other vets were in her office, but one was on vacation, and the other one was doing house calls. He dealt with large animals and was off looking at horses and some llamas today. All in all, it worked. They shared the surgical days, and often they would book a separate day each, depending on what they had to deal with.

Realizing everything was done, Holly grabbed her favorite sweater and her purse, waited with Mittle for Bettina, one of her techs, to finish up, and the three women walked out together. With the doors locked securely behind them, Holly walked over to her small SUV and hopped in. She sat there for a long moment before she started up the engine. The other two girls got in their vehicles and took off.

She looked at her phone. No messages from Zane. She backed up with the intent of heading home when his truck pulled in.

He pulled up beside her, rolled down his window so

they were face-to-face and said, "Just got back from Reggie's. We found the shepherd, and he's been treated this afternoon. I'm going back tomorrow morning."

"Good," she said, her heart light. "Want to come to my place for dinner?"

He hesitated.

She shook her head. "You don't have anywhere else to go. You're well on your way to completing your mission. Surely you can have dinner with a friend."

"Do you need any groceries?" he asked.

She considered the issue. "It wouldn't hurt to pick up a couple steaks. I've got vegetables, but I don't know that I have enough meat."

"Let's go there first then."

She nodded. "Follow me." She waited until he turned around to come up behind her, then she took a right onto the main road and headed down to the small mall. A large supermarket was in town, but she preferred the butcher shop. It stocked more organic foods. She was lucky she made decent money and could afford it, although it wasn't something she did all the time. For whatever reason, tonight she wanted to make a nice dinner, and that meant some of the better pieces of meat.

She pulled into the mall parking lot, waited until he pulled up beside her, and the two of them walked into the butcher's together. There she picked up two nice cuts of marbled beef that were every bit of an inch and a half thick. She paid for them, even though he tried.

"Let's walk over to the other side." A bakery was part of the small exclusive store, and she chose a loaf of French bread.

When she walked to get veggies, she realized he was no

longer with her. Frowning, she picked up salad greens, knowing she already had potatoes. She also had broccoli and cauliflower, if he wanted more veggies.

With all her purchases paid for and bagged, she walked back to the SUV, seeing him walking out of the nearby liquor store with several bottles of wine in his arms.

She smiled. "Did you get a nice red?"

"Got a couple," he said. "If you won't let me help with groceries, the least I can do is pick up a bottle or two."

She laughed. "You know the way back to my place?" She told him the address.

He turned around, considered their location, then nodded. "Yes, I do. I'll see you there."

She hopped into her vehicle and drove home. She wasn't surprised to see him behind her most of the way. After parking in her driveway, she unloaded the groceries and headed into the kitchen.

"Need some help?" he asked.

"I'd love to see these barbecued, and I'm not a great hand at that. How are you with a grill?"

"Excellent," he said, walking out to the deck. He checked the propane, while she watched, then opened the lid and asked, "Medium rare still?"

It warmed her heart that he remembered. "Perfect. I'll put on some potatoes, so how about I give you the word when they are almost done, and then you can start the steaks?"

The grill looked a bit dirty, so he scrubbed it down as he waited. When she gave him the word, he tossed on the steaks, while she made the salad. In companionable silence, they worked together until he called out to say the steaks were done. She already had the table set and the wine for him to open.

When they sat down, she sniffed the air and smiled. "I do love a barbecued steak."

"I do too," he said. He smiled at the dinner as a whole. "This brings back a lot of good memories."

"Good," she said quietly. "I'm glad to hear that. I'd hate to think you only had bad memories."

"I don't have too many negative memories," he said. "It was quite a few years ago now."

"Four or five at least," she admitted. "I was married to Brody for two years, and he's been gone for two years now." "How are you handling his loss?"

"I think I'm there," she said quietly. "Some people might find that fast, but I'm not so sure."

He was about finished with his steak when his phone rang. He pulled it out and said, "Hey, Reggie. How is the shepherd doing?"

Holly could hear Reggie's frazzled voice coming through the phone.

"I'm not so sure how the dog's doing," he said. "My clinic was broken into and somebody tried to get at him."

Zane stood and put his phone on Speaker. "You're saying somebody broke into the clinic to get Katch?"

"Yes," Reggie said. "Anytime animals are here overnight, somebody stays, and that was me tonight. Honestly, I was grateful because I was so damn tired. It's been a long day. But, about ten minutes ago, somebody snuck through the front, set off the alarms, and, with the sirens blaring, bolted into the back, searching for the dog. I don't think he expected anyone to be here. When I came out, he fired at me, the little bastard." Reggie's voice strengthened with the power of shock. "Then he took off."

"But you think he was after the shepherd?"

"Absolutely. He was drawing a bead on him, even as the dog was in the cage, sleeping. Although he's not sleeping now, not with the alarm going off."

"Did you call the cops?" Zane asked, pacing the kitchen.

"Yes," he said. "I did."

"ARE THEY COMING out there now?" Zane said, "Do you want me to come too?"

Reggie hesitated. "I don't know what to say to that. Part of me says, I want you to come because you look like you could handle yourself in this situation. I handle wounds and sutures. I don't deal with guns. The cops are on their way, but I doubt they'll stay all night. The security is once again set, so that much is done. But honestly, I don't know if I'll sleep a wink. As far as the shepherd, I had to give him a sedative to calm him down."

"Wow," Zane said, running his hand through his hair. "I expected this, planned to sit in your parking lot later tonight, but I didn't think the hunter would come this soon."

Reggie said, "I surely didn't. Not sure exactly what the hell is going on with this dog, but the bottom line is, it's still an injured animal, and this is probably the guy who shot him in the first place. I don't know why he can't leave well enough alone, but I suspect he'll be back, and I doubt he'll take no for an answer next time. He didn't shoot me, and he didn't shoot you, but ..." He let his voice trail off.

"I know," Zane said, pacing about the dining table now. "I definitely got the impression that, in any other circumstance, he would have shot me but not out in that field today."

"Yeah," Reggie said with feeling. "I've got to tell you. I feel the same way."

"I'm coming over," Zane said. "I'm with Holly right now, but I'm only twenty minutes away."

"It wouldn't hurt to have you give me a hand checking over the shepherd. At the moment he's fine, but I'm having trouble keeping him calm."

"Okay. I'm coming now," Zane said. "Hold on." He pocketed his phone and looked at Holly. "I'm sorry but I've got to go."

She'd already cleaned up the table and had her sweater on. "I'm coming with you," she said. "Reggie sounds pretty frazzled. He might need an extra hand with Katch." He frowned, and she just walked to the door. "Don't argue."

Once in his truck she asked, "Why would somebody continue to hunt down the dog?"

"I don't know," he said. "No good reason comes to mind."

A moment later she spoke hesitantly. "I hate to even ask, but what kind of bad reasons come to mind?"

"Revenge, a game, hunting a trophy. I don't know," he said. "In normal circumstances, the dog could have attacked somebody, and they've come to make sure it's gone and won't hurt another person. But the hunter's already shot Katch twice, or at least somebody has shot him twice—whether it's this guy or not, I don't know. For all we know, three men are involved, and two didn't manage to get their kill, and this guy's determined to beat the other two."

"That's horrible," she cried out.

"Sometimes people are horrible, remember?"

"Not the men in my life," she said firmly.

He laughed at that. "My father is hardly a nice, warm, welcoming man."

"True, but he won't torture an animal."

"No," Zane said quietly. "He'd shoot him between the eyes before it got to that point."

CHAPTER 5

"DO YOU HATE your father?" Holly asked.

"No. I have no feelings for him whatsoever," Zane said. "I had a shitty childhood. Lost my mother early. Never really knew my father but lost all chance at that when he just withdrew after her death. As brothers, we were on our own at that point. The three of us grew up hating each other—maybe my brothers were vying for Dad's attention? I have no clue. But it's very unfortunate because, even as adults, there is no connection between us. Obviously Brody and Butch had a relationship of some kind with my father. I didn't, and maybe I missed out on that earlier version of Dad. I do know nothing's there now for me and Dad," he said honestly.

"But that could change when you break down some of the walls between you," she said. "It doesn't have to stay this way."

"Maybe not," he said. "But what's the incentive to change it? Dad doesn't care. It's Brody he lost, who he cared about. He always made that clear to both Butch and me."

"Do you think it affected Butch the same way?"

"I don't know. It's possible. But, at the same time, I think it's more a case of Butch being older. He already had time with Dad and Mom. Or maybe he's more like Dad and handles it differently than I do. But I was the middle child, the *troubled child*. According to my father, I wouldn't listen, and I had a mind of my own. Since I was close to my mother, I never really connected with my father. After she died, things between my dad and me just got worse.

"He *really* didn't want me to go into the military, which never made any sense to me. It's not like I joined a cult or something. Although he was against pretty much *everything* I did. I think he was just being contrary to make my life as miserable as his was. He might even have hated me just because I moved on after Mom died.

"When I enlisted in the navy, my father washed his hands of me. I guess he saw that as his final dominion over me. The line between a dependent child and an independent adult. Whatever. I have no idea how his addled mind thinks. I've just been searching for answers to stop those questions from rambling around endlessly in my own mind. Regardless, to him, it seemed as if me going into the navy was the final straw, and he wanted nothing more to do with me after that."

"In some ways, I can understand," she said, "because I was pretty upset too."

"And yet, I never said anything about you going to vet school. That seven-year commitment would impact *my* life too. What difference did it make if I was in the navy while you were in vet school?"

"Oddly enough, I was just thinking that today," she said with a half laugh. "Back then I obviously wasn't mature enough to hear what you were trying to say."

"It really bothered you that I was going to the navy?"

"Not about the joining-the-navy part. But about leaving me, yes," she said. "I never thought about the fact that you were going to serve our country. So many others didn't either. All I could see was the fact that you wouldn't be here for me."

"But you weren't going to be here for me either," he said, a question in his voice. "You would be buried in schoolwork and not even in town during the week, only coming home on weekends. So what difference did it make?"

"Back then it made a difference. I wanted you here when I was," she said. "I don't expect you to understand. I can't even really explain it, but it made a difference."

"Apparently you kept on with your life's goal, and I went on with my life's goal," he said, "so whatever."

"I think it was a major contributor to our breakup," she said. "We just didn't see enough of each other."

"If it was meant to be, you'd think we would have made it through that period though," he said. "We managed for a couple years. Then it seemed like, whenever I came home, you didn't give a damn. So, when I left, it was more a case of *Why did I even bother coming for a visit?*"

"I cared," she said. "But, as soon as I saw you again, I was already girding myself for when you would leave. It was incredibly hard to know you would leave again. It was almost easier when you were gone for long stints. I didn't have to deal with the emotions and the sense of abandonment."

"I'm sorry," he said after a moment's silence. "I never thought of that."

She shrugged. "And I never thought how you felt when I went off and became a vet either. It's what I always wanted to do," she confessed.

"I know," he said, "and that's why I didn't worry about it. I always wanted to go into the navy too."

"And yet, your father said it was a sudden decision," she said. "And I don't remember you ever talking about it."

"I never talked about it because it would never be acceptable to Dad. My father never, ever wanted me to go, and my brothers would just laugh at me as they always had."

"Butch too?"

"Butch most of all," he said. "In a way I think Brody understood the most."

"I think he did too," she said softly. "He always spoke highly of you. He admired your decision. But then he also admired the fact that you would buck up against your dad."

"There was nothing to admire," Zane said, his tone weary. "It was one fight after another. No one won. I couldn't have stayed much longer. And you weren't ready to take the next step in our relationship, so I needed to do something for me, and that was joining the navy."

"So then what went wrong?"

"We grew apart. We both wanted different things," he said. "You insisted I stay home, and I wasn't sure what you were doing when I was gone. You were always with Brody and his friends."

She gasped. "Are you saying you think I cheated on you?"

He slid her a glance. "You hooked up with Brody very, very quickly." Her face paled as he studied her.

"I did *not* cheat on you," she said. "Where would you even get that idea?"

He stared out the window. "My father. He told me that you were already seeing Brody and that you two were a better match, that I should just get the hell out and stay out."

She gasped hard, and he could hear her holding back sobs.

"Look. I'm sorry," he said. "That was a long time ago. I

didn't mean to bring it all up again."

"Obviously not long enough," she said, wiping her eyes with the back of her hand. "I never cheated on you. I never went out with Brody until we broke it off. Sure, we all hung out together, but we never dated. And I didn't even like him in the beginning. But he insisted on keeping me company. Your father, however, was very supportive."

"Yeah, that would be my dad," he said. "In the meantime, he told me that I needed to butt out so the two of you could have a decent life together. He told me that you two had already been seeing each other, but you felt guilty because I was in the military, and you didn't want to break it off with me. Yet you worried because God only knows what I was doing at the time," he said in frustration. "Believe me. Dad let me know quite clearly that I was the one in the way."

"Is that why you didn't get along with Brody? I don't know what exactly happened back then," she said, "but, for the longest time, I was so angry, so mad at you that I was happy to go out with Brody, if just to stick it to you," she admitted. "I did say I was young, right?"

"Absolutely," he said. "And my rage was all because I figured you were cheating on me with him."

"But I wasn't. I'm surprised you even came back to see us when you were on leave."

"I couldn't help myself," he said. "Besides, he was still my brother and about the only one who would talk to me."

"Back then your father was friendly when we were all together," she said, "wasn't he?"

"He was to a certain extent," Zane said. "But I think it was only to make sure I kept away from you guys the way he wanted. He was very happy when you two got married."

"Amazing," she said. "I wonder why he didn't like you and me together."

"Because he didn't like me," Zane said. "Don't ever think differently. He might tell you something else, but the bottom line is, I was his least-favorite son. And he liked you, wanted you for one of them, and Brody seemed to be it. I think Butch and Sandra were a good mix. Although Butch is turning out to be more like Dad every time I see him."

"I'm not sure you should tell either of them that," she said on a half laugh.

Just then the intersection light turned, and he made a left turn, heading toward Reggie's clinic. "Maybe," he said. "The thing is, my father has been a very negative force in my life. And I really don't want to be here with him. I came for the dog, but I'm leaving as soon as I can." When an odd silence filled his vehicle, he turned and looked at her. "What?"

"Oh, nothing," she said. "Those words just bring back all kinds of bad memories about how, as soon as you arrived, all I could worry about was the fact that you were leaving again. That's been our entire relationship. It's a fact that you come, and then you go, and I'm left dealing with the aftermath of emotions."

"But, in this case," he said, "it's nothing to be worried about. Because we don't have a relationship." He heard her startled gasp and winced at his own harsh wording. "Look. I didn't mean it that way. I just meant, we're not together, and you were married to my brother."

"Is that a life sentence to you?" She motioned at intersection ahead. "Turn left to get to Reggie."

"What are you talking about?" he asked, making the turn.

"You said I was married to your brother, as if that's a life sentence, as if that's something that can't ever be walked past," she said. "Your brother's dead. I have moved forward. He's always going to be there in my life, but it's almost as if, because I married your brother, there's no such thing as having a relationship with you again."

"I don't know that there is," he said. "There would have to be a big adjustment on my part. And I don't know how I'd feel about something like that."

"Maybe you should take another look at it," she said, "because who knows? Maybe you'll open yourself up to seeing what's still there between us."

He pulled into the parking lot of Reggie's clinic and turned off the engine. "Is something still there?"

"Absolutely," she said. She looked at him, opened the passenger door and hopped out, walking around to the front.

He shoved his hands in his pockets. "What?" He studied her face in the darkness.

"Of course there's something between us," she said in disgust. "I'd hoped that the years away wouldn't have stopped you from being honest."

"I'm always honest."

"Then, in this case, you're being thick," she snapped. She headed toward the front door, but, instead of ringing the bell, she pulled out her phone and called Reggie.

Zane watched her. "Are you saying you want to rekindle things between us?"

"I don't know. Right now I think you should disappear and stay disappeared," she snapped. "It's easier than watching you walk into my life and turn around and walk back out again. That's something I can't tolerate."

"I'm not in the navy anymore," he snapped right back.

"So what difference does it make?"

She glared at him. "None at all. And this is a stupid conversation."

Just then the door in front of them opened, and Reggie let them in.

REGGIE LOOKED AT the two of them suspiciously, his gaze going from one to the other. "You two fighting?"

Zane shot him a hard look as he stepped inside and passed him. "Not really. Just different viewpoints."

"We're fighting," Holly announced. "Forget what he said."

Reggie chuckled. "Obviously you two know each other."

"Yes," Zane said, his voice tight. "Maybe too much."

Holly glared at him, but he ignored it.

"Where the hell are the cops?" Zane asked.

"Some attempted bank robbery delayed them. Since I told them that you were on your way and how the intruder was gone and that I'm not injured, they said they may wait until the morning."

"So take us through what happened," Zane said.

Reggie launched into an explanation, leading them to his office, where he had set up a cot in a small side room. "I sleep here at night, so I can check on the animals. The shepherd was in a bad way, so I stayed here overnight. Somewhere around ten o'clock, I heard the alarms go off. I hopped up and went to shut them off, but the intruder had already made it inside. He was heading toward the cages, and that's in the opposite end of the building." He pointed out where the security station was and how the intruder had to travel through the reception area to the back, then through the treatment rooms to the surgery room and into the rooms in the back where they dealt with the animals after surgeries.

"I was heading toward the dog when I came through the other treatment room. I just instinctively knew this had to do with the poor shepherd. The intruder had a rifle out, looking at each of the cages, and realized only one of the large cages had a clipboard hanging from it. He dropped down, took a look at the clipboard. The dog started to growl, and the gunman said, 'There you are, you bastard.' When he lifted the rifle, I popped on the lights and said, 'Hey, what the hell are you doing?' Thankfully he didn't kill me right then," Reggie admitted.

"I didn't even think of that. I just wanted to stop him from hurting the shepherd any more than he had, and I'd already put a lot of time and effort into helping him get better. The intruder took one look at me, and he bolted out the back door. I went outside to see where he was, but he was gone. I did hear a vehicle spitting gravel as it ripped out of the side street." He pointed to where the clinic property stopped at a corner, where a side street connected to the main road.

"I don't know if that was him or not, but it seemed logical. When I came back in, I did a thorough search around the rest of the clinic, but he left nothing here and took nothing from here. We have had break-ins in the past, where people have come in after drugs," he said with emotion as he looked over at Holly. "I'm sure you've had that trouble too."

"Absolutely," she said. "And it's worse in a poor economy. Because a lot of people think they can sell these drugs for easy cash. I haven't had a break-in in a while though."

"Neither had I," Reggie admitted. "But that was my first

thought. When I saw the gun and him heading for the shepherd, I thought, *Jesus, it's him.*"

"So he didn't take anything, and he didn't attempt to look at anything else?" Zane asked.

"No," he said, "not that I could tell." He ran his fingers over his balding head and sighed. "I really could have used a few more hours' sleep, but I'm far too wide awake now."

"It's still early," Zane said. "If we can make sure everything's secure and get your alarm set, I doubt he'll be back tonight."

Reggie frowned. "I honestly don't want to keep the shepherd here if that gunman is coming back after him."

"How badly hurt is he?" Holly asked. "I could move him to my clinic."

Reggie looked at her hopefully. "That would help, if the gunman knew the dog had been moved. At the moment, as far as he's concerned, the dog is here, and this is where he'll come back to."

"True enough," Zane said. "But we're dealing with two things. One, him coming back, and two, him coming back and actually finding Katch. We don't want the gunman to find this dog, so if we move Katch, that's one thing. Somehow we need to post a notice saying something about the dog not being here. But that would require an awful lot of explanation for a lot of people."

"Yeah," Reggie said moodily, staring at the large cage that held the dog.

"Did you knock him out again?"

"I had to," he said. "He shouldn't have been awake in the first place, but it must've been instinct, knowing he was in danger again."

"Good," Holly said. "If we had a way to move him, I'd

say we take him back to the clinic and get him safely installed in one of my cages. I can keep an eye on him at work."

"We also have to make sure nobody sees us doing this," Zane said. "We don't want this gunman to come to your clinic either."

"If Katch is gone, the gunman won't know where Katch went, will he?" Holly asked.

"How about the two of you decide how is the best way to transfer the shepherd," Zane said, "while I go make sure that asshole really is gone." And on that note he turned and headed out the back door.

Outside, he stopped and sniffed the air. It contained a mixture of pain, fear and gasoline. He sniffed again. It was almost as if he could smell the gunpowder. Giving his head a shake, he walked around to the back area where he'd already been more than once today. And then he checked the parking lot front and back and walked around to the corner of the side street where the vehicle had supposedly been parked. It was obvious a vehicle had recently left because gravel was spit up on the sidewalk and along the path before it. The tracks were there but hard to see because the driver had let the tires spin. Whether that was a deliberate move to hide his tracks, Zane didn't know, but it was a smart move nonetheless.

He walked around the neighborhood, going out three blocks, checking to make sure nobody was waiting. He found nothing suspicious. None of the houses appeared to have direct access to the clinic itself, so it wasn't like somebody was in a house watching him.

As he walked back to Reggie's, Zane gazed around at the immediate area. It was a busy street with easy access from two sides of the clinic, and then, with the side street at the back, that made it easy for anybody coming in that direction too. Good for a business sense but even nicer for somebody skulking around in the shadows. A lot of escape routes were here.

Zane slowly made his way back to where the two vets were talking. As he walked in, Reggie stepped out, his face worried. And then he saw Zane, and relief washed over his features. "For a moment there," Reggie said, "I thought you were the other guy."

"The other guy is gone," Zane said. "I doubt he'll be back tonight."

"I don't want him back at all," Reggie said. "I wish I had a photograph of him to warn my staff."

"If you had a photograph," Zane said, "I would have an easier time tracking him down."

"There aren't even cameras along this street," Reggie said.

"What about your security system?" Holly said. "Do you have video?"

He nodded. "And I checked it. Got nothing on the intruder."

"Did you figure out how to move the shepherd?"

"Yeah," she said, looking at him sideways. "In the back of your truck with me keeping an eye on him."

He frowned at her. "That's hardly a good idea, is it?"

"We can move him on blankets."

"We take him on a gurney out of here, transport him into the bed with blankets," Reggie said. "And then repeat the process at your end."

"How many tubes, catheters, etc., does he have, and does he have to keep them in for the trip?" Zane asked.

Reggie shook his head. "We'll unclip them, or you can take the bag and hold it, if you want. Otherwise, for fifteen to twenty minutes, he'll be okay. We've already got the lines in. You can rehook him up when you get to Holly's."

"In that case, any reason I can't just pick him up and carry him out and put him in the back of the truck, and you can keep an eye on him?"

"In the pickup bed?" she asked.

"Are you sure you can lift him?" Reggie asked.

Zane just looked at the two of them.

Holly shrugged. "Whatever you want to do."

He walked back out to his truck and checked out the bed. The pickup bed was big enough that it might be the easiest answer. He popped down the tailgate, not liking the fact there was no canopy, then went to the double cab and opened up the door to the back seat.

As Holly came up beside him, she asked, "Why don't we lay him on the bench seat in the front, and I'll sit in the back?"

"I was just thinking that," he said. He moved her purse to the back. He walked around, closed the tailgate again and headed back inside the clinic.

Reggie, using the blankets, had gently moved the shepherd out of the cage so he lay in the center of the floor.

"As long as it's not dangerous to move him," Zane said, "I'm okay to try this. But I don't want him injured by us moving him."

"Neither do we," Holly said.

Zane reached down and gently slid a hand under Katch's chest and another under his hips, and ever-so-carefully rose, carrying him out. With Reggie hovering like a nursemaid, Zane quickly walked out to the pickup. He awkwardly laid the dog on the large bench seat in the front. He hadn't even considered the fact he had a bench seat in the rental because almost all of them had single seats. But, for this purpose, it was a very welcome design feature.

He closed the door, turned and shook Reggie's hand. "Thanks for looking after him."

Reggie raised his hands in surrender. "Not like I had much chance to," he said, turning to look back. "I guess at this point, I can lock up and go home, grab a few hours' sleep in my own bed. I think I even have a cancellation in the morning. I could possibly get some real rest."

"Do that," Holly said, getting into the back seat of Zane's truck. "We'll be fine."

Zane walked around to the front of the truck, hopped into the driver's seat and gently pulled the vehicle forward. "How's he doing?"

"He's holding," Holly said. "This isn't the best way to transport an injured animal, but our options are fairly limited."

"If there was a canopy on the bed," he said, "I would have put him back there. And you could have ridden beside him, but, without that to keep you two from the wind, it wasn't a good idea."

She didn't say much as he drove to her clinic. Every time he checked on her though, she was monitoring the dog, and he appreciated that.

He soon saw her clinic and pulled up to the door. "Let's get him inside as quickly as we can."

Holly hopped out and said, "I'll go open up."

And she disappeared from sight.

CHAPTER 6

S HE UNLOCKED THE front door to the clinic, shut off
the alarm, moved into the rear surgery room and pulled
out a gurney. Zane would probably argue, but it was still the
easiest way to move the dog. She opened up a cage so it was
ready, just in case Zane was already coming with Katch.

As she turned around, pushing the gurney, Zane came
in. "I can put him on the gurney if you need to hook him
up. Otherwise it's easier to put him directly into the cage."

"The gurney, please."

He gently laid Katch on the gurney and stepped back
while she checked him over. She had the notes from Reggie
on the dog's care. When she finally straightened with
satisfaction, she said with a bright smile, "He's no worse for
wear. Let me get an IV going and some pain meds before he
wakes up on us."

"Yeah, that's not what we need right now," he said. "He
needs to be kept calm and quiet, I'd presume, to not pull out
any of his stitches or to restart the bleeding."

"Absolutely," she said.

He stood and watched, waiting as she reset the IV, then
she looked at him. "Now I need help getting him into the
cage."

Together they gently maneuvered the dog inside, then
closed and locked the door. She grabbed a report sheet and

wrote down what had happened and when and why. Then she hooked it under the cage. "He'll be fine for at least four hours. Now I'm facing the same problem Reggie had."

"What's that?" He looked at her steadily.

She glanced at her watch. "It's after midnight. I'm staying here with the dog."

He nodded. "Then I'll stay too."

"No, you don't have to," she said. "I've only got one bed here anyway."

"That's fine," he said. "I don't need a bed."

"Why are you staying?"

"Because we don't know that we weren't followed. I don't want an intruder coming in while you're sleeping, hurting you and Katch."

She could feel the color draining from her face. "Fine," she admitted painfully. "I wouldn't want that to happen either. But I need sleep. I've got a full day again tomorrow."

"Go for it," he said, motioning toward her office. "I hope you have a cot, and you can actually sleep."

"I do, but it's not the most comfortable thing. However, I am tired, and I've got surgery in the morning."

"Then you better get at it," he said. "I'll make myself comfortable out in the reception room."

"That big long bench is in there," she said doubtfully, staring in the direction. "But it wasn't meant to be slept on."

"Doesn't matter," he said. "I'll be fine."

She just stared at him hard.

He shrugged. "What do you want me to say? I was in the navy and slept under much worse conditions. It's all good."

When she didn't move, he shrugged. "You're wasting sleeping time."

She brushed past him and headed to her office, but he

stepped in behind her. "Hang on. I'll make sure your office is clear."

She hadn't even thought of that. She waited while he did a quick sweep, even opening up the closet and storage cupboard.

Then he turned and asked, "Where's the cot?" She walked to the cupboard, moved aside something in front of her and pulled out the cot, which she flipped open. Then she grabbed blankets off the couch across from her desk and said, "I'll be fine here."

He waited a moment, uncertain.

She waved him off. "Go, go, go. I'm fine."

He stepped out of her office and closed the door quietly behind him.

Then she realized she hadn't reset the alarm. She hopped out of the office. "I forgot to reset the alarm." She went through the motions, made sure it was set, then returned to her office. "Good night," she called out, shutting her office door again.

"Good night," he said.

She could hear his voice from the main reception area. There was something odd to it though, something tense. She wondered what his problem was. But she curled up on her cot and pulled a blanket over her shoulders. If she could just grab some sleep, it would help.

She'd spent more than a few nights here, looking after animals. It was part of the job. But the next day was always brutal because trying to get enough sleep for whatever was to come was always hard.

Tonight she had luck on her side. She closed her eyes and fell asleep.

BACK OUT IN the reception room, Zane lay down on the bench and closed his eyes. The bench didn't quite hold his wide shoulders, so he had to settle in at a slight angle. But it was a chance to close his eyes and to think about what had just happened.

Why was somebody so dang eager to take out that shepherd? Because that was really what was at the bottom of this. Even though Zane and Reggie each had saved the shepherd from the hunter, now Zane had to make sure this guy didn't come back and try to take him out again. Why would somebody hate a dog so much?

Only if he hurt somebody and hurt them bad enough that they were determined to get revenge.

He frowned at that thought, wondering, because this could be the hunter's reason, driving all his actions.

Zane closed his eyes and let his mind drift, thoughts coming, and thoughts going. When he saw headlights flash in the reception room, he opened his eyes and studied them. Then he heard the sound of a vehicle. Driving slow. The low growl of a truck and a wide slow sweep as the vehicle came into the parking lot, then pulled around to the side.

As soon as the headlights no longer shone in his direction, Zane got up and walked through the office to the side window to see the vehicle. It was already around the corner, so he couldn't see it. He didn't know where it went, but he walked through the surgery area back to where the shepherd was. If it was the same man, he'd already triggered the security system at the other clinic. Was that what he would do here too? And how had he known they were here? He had to have been watching Reggie's clinic or somehow had it bugged and heard their conversation.

But that didn't make any sense. How would the gunman know Katch would return to Reggie's? It was more likely that Zane and Holly had just been seen with Katch. Maybe the intruder had taken off, but he had either come back or driven past and seen Zane's truck sitting here. Which meant the gunman had followed them here. How else would he recognize the rental truck as being used by Zane?

He went from window to window, looking for a way to catch whoever was out there. He wanted to see if he approached the doors. And then he thought about that big pen in the back that led to a fenced yard at Reggie's. Zane headed toward the rear of Holly's clinic and stopped when he heard a sound on the other side of one of the doors back there. Did Holly have a treatment room that led out to a pen too, just like at Reggie's? Because, if she did, that would make the most sense for the hunter to come in through there.

It might have been locked, but was it wired into the same security system? He doubted it. More often than not, the front and back doors and the bigger windows were done, but something like a pen door would have been missed.

He leaned up against the wall next to the door where he expected the intruder and waited. Zane heard footsteps, and then the doorknob in front of him turned. When the door was pulled inward, and a man stepped in, Zane jumped him. He grunted, but Zane wasn't prepared to have *any* kind of a real fight with a coward who kills dogs with a gun. Zane knocked him out instantly. Then he turned on the lights and checked out the intruder. And, sure enough, he had a weapon in his hand. Zane kicked that free, rolled the man over and checked his pockets for ID.

John McAfee. It gave an address and phone number.

Zane snapped pictures of it with his phone. He knew the cops would do the same and go much further but that didn't mean they'd share that information. Afterward he put everything back in John's wallet and put it back in the man's pocket. A further check revealed nothing else except for the handgun. Then he took photos of McAfee's face. Knowing at some point he would come to, Zane looked around for rope or something, opened several drawers, and then he heard Holly.

"Zane, is that you?"

He called out, "Yes. Do you have any zap straps here?"

"Zap straps? What for?" came her sleepy reply. She stepped out of her office, coming toward him.

He could hear her soft padded feet on the floor.

When she came into the lit treatment room, she gasped. "Oh, my God! Where did he come from?"

He pointed at the door the man was still half in. "I presume that leads to an outside fenced yard."

She stared at Zane, stared at the intruder and nodded slowly. "Yes, it does."

"And it's not wired into your security system?"

"No. You're right, it's not connected to the security system. We never thought it would be necessary."

"How about now?" he asked, watching her still struggling with the concept. He nudged her with a reminder. "Zap straps?"

"Yes, of course," she said and walked over to another cupboard and handed him a bag.

He zipped two together and then secured the intruder's wrists behind his back. Zane lifted McAfee and put him in a chair; then Zane strapped both his feet together and then again strapped them to one leg of the chair. No point tying one ankle to each side of the chair because it was too damn easy to then just waddle side to side. So Zane clipped them together to one side and then stood back and belted him across the face. He heard Holly's gasp. "Do you want him to wake up or what?"

"I want to call the police," she snapped.

"Go ahead," he said, "feel free." Somebody would have to take this asshole off her hands. He watched as she stepped a few feet away so she could call the cops.

While she was talking, the man groaned. Knowing he would be out of time soon enough, Zane squatted in front of him and said, "Hey, wake up."

The man groaned again, opened bleary eyes to stare at him. He frowned, looked around, saw where he was and started to swear.

"Yeah, I'd be swearing too if I was stuck in a surgery room like this. Too bad we don't have a psychopath veterinarian to cut off your balls and make you eat them," Zane said casually. "Or maybe we don't need a veterinarian at all. I can play the psychopath and serve you your balls. Because, man, torture is a hell of a way to get answers."

The guy just stared at him, his face twisting in anger, but there was no fear.

"Military background?" Zane asked.

One eyebrow rose, but he didn't answer.

Zane nodded. "Yeah, military. Probably drummed out for bad behavior and a shitty attitude."

The man's face leaned forward, but he didn't show any expression.

"So what have you got against that dog?" Zane asked conversationally. "That's a War Dog. He deserves a decent life after getting shipped home."

"He shouldn't be alive," the man snapped. "Maybe not today, maybe not tomorrow, but I'll kill him soon enough," he said.

"And why is that?"

But the man wouldn't explain.

"You got some beef with him from wartime or since he came back? He just wants to have a life of peace."

"He should be shot."

"We already know your attitude on that," Zane said. "But now you've broken into two different clinics. You've shot at the animal several times, and you haven't managed to kill him."

"I want him to suffer first."

"Like he made somebody else suffer? Is that where this is going? An eye for an eye?"

The man gave a half a shrug.

Zane studied his body language for a moment and then said, "Did he hurt somebody? Somebody you cared about?"

His lip curled.

Zane persisted. "The question is whether it was during wartime or since he came back."

"He's a War Dog, isn't he?"

"So you actually know this dog from over there?" Zane was amazed. "What are the odds of that?"

"It happens," he snapped. "Some of these dogs just need to be shot right from the beginning."

"Like the Vietnam War Dogs. We really treated them well, didn't we? After doing years and years of service for us, saving our sorry asses, we turned around and killed them, rather than bring them home and give them decent lives."

It still pissed him off to think about how the military had treated those animals. They'd given their all, and all they'd gotten was a piece of lead as a gift afterward.

"So what did he do? Miss out on a mission? Was he a bomb-sniffing dog, and he missed a bomb or something?"

The intruder just stared at Zane sullenly.

"Was it a friend or a brother?" At the flicker in McAfee's eye, Zane nodded. "Brother then."

The gunman remained silent for a short moment. "It doesn't fucking matter," the intruder said. "The dog's as good as dead."

"Well, after coming into this place with a weapon," Zane said, "I'm sure the cops have something to say to you."

"Doesn't matter. Even if I'm there for a few weeks, big deal," he said. "The dog's still dead."

Just then Holly came back in. "It's not the dog's fault. Whatever beef you have with whatever happened in the war, it's not the dog that sent your brother over there. It's not the dog that's responsible for your brother being kept over there. And it's not the dog that was responsible for your brother going out on a mission. So stop blaming the dog for something that he had no control over."

CHAPTER 7

HOLLY HATED TO see anybody blaming an animal when it was obviously people who were responsible. The dog may not have been able to save someone or may have startled someone or something out on a mission that had caused a big blowup, but it still wasn't the animal's fault. People had sent the animal out there, and people had sent other people out there. The blame needed to be placed where it belonged.

She looked at Zane and said, "The cops are on their way. They should be here any moment."

He nodded and motioned toward the guy in the chair. "Do you know who he is?"

She shook her head. "No clue."

"So he's not from around here?"

She shrugged. "I have no idea."

Zane studied him. "Are you from around here?"

The man shrugged. "None of your business."

"I've already checked your wallet," Zane said, crossing his arms, leaning back against the counter. "It gives me an address, but that doesn't mean that's where you're currently living."

The man's gaze narrowed. "You had no business going through my wallet."

"You had no business pulling a gun on us," Holly said in a heated tone. "Nor shooting a dog. Nor breaking and entering two separate clinics. For all I know you were after drugs."

The man spat on the floor. "I don't want your fucking drugs," he said. "No way I need those."

"Says you," Zane said, shifting comfortably against the counter. "I highly doubt the police will believe you. You hit two vet clinics on the same night. As far as I'm concerned, you're after drugs. I'm sure they can add a couple extra charges to your sheet for that."

The gunman glared at him.

"Did you shoot those other dogs?" Holly asked curiously.

Confused, he shook his head. "Only one dog I know of that needs killing."

She shared a look with Zane.

Too bad. It would be nice to know the same man had done all the shootings. Still, it was an unfortunate side of life that some people hated dogs and would take them out anytime they had the opportunity.

In the distance, sirens could be heard. As Holly left for the front door, she called out, "Are you okay being alone with him?"

Zane called after her, "I'm fine. I hope he does try to escape."

"You leave him alone," she ordered. "I don't want you hauled away to jail too."

"Not happening," he said.

She shut off the alarm system as the cops pulled in the parking lot. She stepped outside, and, when the first uniformed man arrived, she smiled up at him. "Am I glad to see you."

"What's going on here?" he asked.

She led the way into the back of the clinic, explaining what had happened.

As they walked in and saw Zane sitting there with the intruder tied to a chair, the first cop hitched his pants up and said, "Well, isn't this an interesting situation."

"I figure he was after drugs," Zane said calmly. "He hit two different vet clinics in the same night."

That wiped the smile off the cop's face. "We don't need another rash of those," he said.

"I wasn't after the damn drugs," the intruder said. "I wanted the dog dead."

The cop just looked at him and frowned. "What's your beef with the dog?"

But the intruder wouldn't say a word.

The second cop hauled McAfee to his feet.

Zane reached down with his knife and cut off the zap straps on the chair and on McAfee's ankles, so he could walk. "I suggest cuffing him at both ends." He pointed to the weapon on the floor. "That's his."

"Shit," the first cop said. He bagged the weapon and led the intruder out to the patrol car.

A second vehicle was out there now, and two more men appeared in the parking lot. They stood around discussing what was going on, and then one of them came inside the clinic to talk to Holly. "Do you want to give your statement now?"

She nodded. "I do, indeed. And then I need to sleep. I have surgery all day tomorrow. I've called one of my assistants in, now that it's safe here, so I can go home and sleep for a few hours."

It took forty minutes to go over everything. When she was finally done, the cop nodded and said, "I'll get this ready for you to sign. Can you stop by tomorrow after work?"

She nodded. "That I can do."

He turned to look at Zane. "How about you? Can you come by at the same time?"

She stepped forward. "We'll come together."

"And what about the dog?" the officer said. "I want to know what the hell's going on with that dog."

"Me too," Zane said. "He's a retiree from the War Dogs program. I came here to make sure he was okay at a request from the military."

At the sound of that, the officer's frown deepened. "Jesus, like we don't have enough of our own animal problems. We got to bring them back from the war with health problems too."

"Which is why I'm making sure he's taken care of," Holly said. "And then we can find the proper place for him."

The officer shook his head as he walked out of the office. "Good luck with that," he said. "If I hear he's dangerous at all, you know what'll happen."

"And then you'll find out why he's dangerous," Zane said, his voice hard. "And who the hell has been abusing him."

The cop turned and looked at Zane. "He's been abused?"

"Abused and shot twice," he said.

At that the cop winced. "He should have killed him clean. No need to hurt an animal like that. I'll see you both tomorrow." And he walked out.

Just then Bettina walked in, and Holly explained, adding, "Katch is sleeping, and I'll be back in a few hours." She grabbed her purse and turned to Zane. "Please take me home so I can go to bed. I want to grab at least a few hours. What about you?"

Zane hesitated.

She looked at him. "You might as well crash for whatever's left of the night."

She watched as he glanced at his watch; then he looked up at her and spoke hesitantly. "If you're sure ..."

"Of course I'm sure," she said. "Come on. Let's go." She reset the alarm and locked up the office and headed out to Zane's vehicle.

Inside the truck she said to him, "How long do you think they'll hold him?"

"Not long enough," he said, his tone grim. "He will be back. I just don't know what we're supposed to do about it."

"We need a resolution to this. He can't just keep breaking into our clinics to get at that animal."

"He isn't going to get his hands on that animal," Zane said. "I don't care what Katch did. He needs our help and the best chance at a good life that we have available to give him."

"A nice fenced yard would be good. Especially one with acreage," she said. "Something like your dad's place."

"Well, that's not a good idea. He'd just as soon put a bullet in him. You know that."

"I didn't say your dad's place. I said *like* your dad's place."

They made the rest of the trip in silence. Before long they pulled up to her house. "I'm really exhausted now," she said. "But, after all this excitement, I don't know if I can sleep."

"You can sleep," he said. "There's nothing to worry about. Just get into bed and let everything fall away."

She led the way into the house. "The spare room's over

there. Follow the hallway and take the first right."

He followed her instructions.

She set her house alarm, locked up and walked down the hall to her bedroom. "We didn't even clean up the kitchen from dinner," she said.

"No time," he said. "I'll do that in the morning."

She barely heard him as she walked into the bathroom, brushed her teeth, stripped off her clothing and crawled under the covers. She shut off the light, and her last thought was that somehow she had managed to get Zane to spend the night. But she sure as hell hoped it didn't take as much panic and chaos to make him stay for the next one. It was nice to have him around.

When she woke the next morning, she rushed through her shower and getting dressed. Zane was downstairs in the kitchen. She looked over at him and smiled brightly. "You didn't have to get up right away," she said.

"Sure I did," he said. "I'm a guest." At her quick frown, he frowned too. As she made coffee, he said, "Are you going to eat breakfast?"

"I need to," she said. "I wasn't kidding about a long day."

"What do you have?" He opened the fridge.

"Sausage patties are in the bottom crisper drawer, if you want to make sausage and toast."

"Absolutely I do," he said, pulling out the stuff. "Do you mind if I cook?"

"Please be my guest," she said in delight. "Then I have a chance to make a lunch to-go."

As he cooked breakfast, she made two big sandwiches.

"Are you going to eat all that today?"

"It's possible," she said. "Sometimes I have to stay late,

and, if I don't take enough food, then it gets hard to keep up my energy."

"Do you have blood sugar issues?"

"If you mean, do I get weak and faint when I don't get enough food? Absolutely. If I'm in surgery for too long, then straighten suddenly, I get dizzy. I just have to look after myself and make sure there's food when I need it." She finished wrapping up her sandwiches. "Do you have any plans for the day?"

"I'm coming with you this morning," he said, "because I want to check on Katch. Then I'll talk to the cops to see what the future is for your intruder."

"Oh, good idea," she said. "Maybe we don't need these sandwiches then. Maybe we should go out for lunch."

"Or we can have lunch in your office," he said. "I can always pick up something."

She shrugged and put the two wrapped sandwiches into a plastic carry bag she used most days. "We'll see," she said. "You can tell me what the cops had to say."

"Good enough," he said. "If you want to grab plates and knives and forks, this is almost ready."

She looked at him in surprise. "That was fast."

He served the plates as the toast popped out of the toaster. He snagged them with one hand and buttered them. "Here you go. Eat up."

She smiled and sniffed the air. "This smells divine."

"Good," he said. "I was afraid you'd be getting up too late, and you'd skip breakfast and take off for work."

"It's certainly happened before," she said, "but I do take special care on surgery days. I have to keep my focus."

"Good to know," he said.

The next few minutes were quiet as they ate.

"You should stop in and see your father today," she said.

"What's the point?"

"Because every time you see him, it'll get a little easier."

"If I'm not staying, what difference will it make?"

"Are you not staying?" she asked, hating the tremor in her voice.

He looked up, then glanced back down at his plate again. "I don't know what I'm doing," he said. "At the moment, I'm a bit of a lost cause."

She gave him a sharp look and shook her head. "Hardly a lost cause. Did you have any training in the military for when you left the navy?"

"I did," he said. "I just haven't decided what I'll do now that I'm out."

"What kind of work were you doing for Titanium Corp?"

"Security mostly," he said, "not exactly what I want to do, but they have lots of jobs. They need the men, so it was a great place to reenter the workforce."

"Have you put much thought into going back to school?"

"No, not really. I don't think I need to either," he said. "I have a few ideas rolling around in my head. I'm just not sure what I want to do."

"Good enough." She hopped to her feet, taking her dishes to the dishwasher. "I have to leave."

He glanced at his watch and saw it was almost eight a.m. "You're early then?"

"No," she said. "Surgery days require more time. I want to be in the right space, not rushing in late before I start."

"Any idea what you're starting with?"

"A lop-eared rabbit. It's coming in to get fixed. He was

breeding stock. He's about to have his mind changed on that subject."

"Poor guy," he said. "Is that the work you do most of the time?"

"A lot of small-animal care is getting them fixed. But also stitches, claws, all kinds of stuff," she said. "There are emergencies, like when animals ingest something not edible. Car accidents bring us, unfortunately, way too much work with broken legs and damaged hips. This afternoon I also have one of the other vets coming in to work on a more complicated case with me. The dog had his leg straightened, but it didn't heal properly. We'll have to rebreak it and pin it at a better angle, so it's more functional."

"Sounds fascinating," he said.

She flashed him a smile as she snagged her purse and sweater. "It can be. It can also be very difficult because we can't save everyone. And I still cry when I lose one."

He nodded, stepping out the front door as she walked out.

"You might as well stay and finish the pot of coffee," she said. "When you get to the clinic, we'll have time enough for you to see the dog."

"I'm coming with you," he said.

She hesitated, then nodded. "If you're ready then, I'll set the alarm."

He stopped on the top step.

She ran through her normal security sequence and then hopped into her SUV. "I'll see you there." And she reversed and headed off at a quick pace.

She knew the longer she waited before going into work, the worse it got. She always needed a few minutes to calm down, have a cup of coffee and relax before she went to look at the first patient. This morning wouldn't be so bad. She was more worried about the Lab's surgery this afternoon. She hadn't set the leg in the first place; another vet had, and the dog was in a lot of pain. Although mobile, every step had to hurt. She wanted to fix the leg properly.

With her mind going through the day's events, the commute to her clinic went quickly, and she pulled into the back of the parking lot to find Mittle's car already there. Inside, Mittle sat behind the reception area. "No matter how early I come," she said, "you always beat me here."

"That's what I'm here for," she said. "Coffee is dripping. Everything looks normal."

"Except for one thing," Holly said. "We had a visitor overnight."

"You mean, the dog in the crate? I figured you must have gotten an emergency call-in."

"Yeah, we did." She explained to Mittle and then described the intruder. "So we have to keep a vigilant eye here." She smiled at Mittle's shocked expression. "Right. In other words, I didn't get a whole lot of sleep. I left Bettina on watch. Is she here?"

"She went to the coffee shop."

"Okay. I'll go grab five in my office. Let me know when our lop-eared rabbit comes in."

"Will do," Mittle said.

Holly grabbed a cup of coffee and headed into her office. At her desk she sat down, put her feet up and let herself relax. Just five minutes. She'd take five minutes to herself, and then she'd start her day.

ZANE WALKED INTO the clinic shortly after Holly. He smiled at Mittle. "I'm here to see Katch. Holly knows I'm here." He nodded toward Holly's office.

Mittle nodded. "I was surprised to hear about the dog. Holly filled me in on the break-in too." She led the way to the back through the surgery room—where two vet assistants were getting things prepped for the day—and on to the room where the animals were kept.

Katch appeared to be awake. He was lying on his side, staring out at the room. Zane walked forward, and the dog just stared at him. He didn't growl. Zane took that as a good sign. He crouched on the floor in front of him and talked to him calmly. He looked at Mittle and asked, "Has he been looked at yet?"

"One of the assistants came through, checked his vitals and IVs, so I know it's all good. Otherwise there would have been a panic when Holly came in," she said. "But the dog looks to be holding his own."

"He had a pretty rough night." Zane hesitated. "It's hard to touch him with the cage locked."

"We keep it that way for safety reasons." Mittle's voice was serious. "To get permission to open it, you'll have to talk to Holly."

"Good enough," he said. "I'll do that."

When she left, he reached down and placed his hand against the cage. "I'm not here to hurt you. I'm actually here to help. But you don't know the difference, do you?"

At the sound of his voice, Katch shifted several times. Zane heard a whimper.

"Are you in pain?" he asked. "I can get somebody to help you with that."

"I'm here to take a look at him," Holly said. "Let me get

close enough." She took the chart, read the new notes from her assistants, then opened the front of the cage. The dog didn't react.

"He's not running for freedom," Zane said.

"No. He's still under sedation, but it looks like he's reacting to the pain a little too much. Let me just increase that dose a bit." She went about changing something on the dog's medications. Finally she stepped back. "He should be fine. I'll check on him in an hour."

"May I sit with him with the gate open for a bit?"

Holly hesitated, then looked at him and back at the dog. "Why?"

"Because I want to touch him," he said. "I want him to feel a human touch that isn't hurting him."

"I can't have him stressed or upset, and I don't want any of his tubes disturbed. So, if he starts to get up, tries to pull away or to fight you, that has to stop immediately. He'll hurt himself. One of the reasons for the extra drugs is to keep him calm and sedated in there."

"And yet, he's not sedated," he said. "His eyes are open, and he was just whimpering."

"The medication should kick in soon," she said. "You can leave the gate open for a few minutes, but, when I come back, I want to see it closed. I can't concentrate on my surgery if I know this cage is open, so you've got five minutes."

He nodded, reached out a hand and gently stroked Katch on top of his head, running his fingers down his nose, gently stroking what should have been soft fur but was instead rough. "He needs a bath," he said softly.

"Well, it's not going to happen here and now," she said from behind him.

Then the door shut, and he turned, realizing he was once again alone. He didn't bother reaching in farther; he just gently stroked the dog's forehead and nose, scratched under his chin. He kept talking to him, always quiet and calm.

When Holly returned a few minutes later, he obediently let her check the dog over, then she closed and locked the gate.

"I'm heading out now," he said. "You take care." He stopped at the door and looked back at her. "Are you okay?"

She looked up at him in surprise. "Of course I'm okay. Why?"

"I just know you're tired," he said. "You're heading into a long day."

"I am," she said with a bright, warm smile. "But, hey, it's not the first time, and it won't be the last time. It's all good."

He gave her a gentle smile. "You don't have to be the tough guy all the time, you know?"

"I'm not," she said with a laugh. "That's up to you guys."

"I'm not a tough guy at all," he said. "I'm a real softy when it comes to dogs."

"You always did have a soft touch with animals."

He nodded. "They usually like me." He cast one more glance at Katch. "Now I'm heading off to the police station to see what they have to say." And, with that, he left, got in his truck and drove the couple blocks to the station.

At the front door, he stepped inside and asked for the cop he'd spoken to last night.

The receptionist nodded and said, "I don't think he's in at the moment. May I leave a message for him?"

He frowned, shoved his hands in his pockets and said,

"This is about the intruder at the vet clinic last night. Actually the intruder at two vet clinics. I want to know what to expect, how dangerous he is, how soon he'll be back on the street and how much danger the clinics are in."

The receptionist frowned. "If you'll take a seat, I'll find out when any of that group are coming in, and maybe I can find somebody to talk to you."

He nodded and headed toward a large bench against the wall. There he sat and quietly waited. When his name was called, he looked up to see it wasn't the cop he'd given his statement to but one of the other men who had escorted the prisoner out. He walked forward, and the officer led him over to his desk.

He pointed at a spare chair. "Take a seat. I thought you weren't coming until this afternoon to sign your statements."

"I'm coming back with the vet at the end of the day," Zane explained. "But we're concerned about the safety of the clinic and the animals and people working there. I thought I'd stop in and see what we could expect from the intruder."

"He's being interviewed this morning, with his lawyer in attendance, and we'll have a better idea of what's going on. He says he was after the dog, not the drugs, and didn't give a damn about the clinic."

"Do you have any laws that stop him from shooting the animal or hurting him?"

"The laws on animal abuse are extremely thin," the cop said. "We're trying to change it, but ..."

"Surely he'll get charged for breaking and entering?"

"Absolutely, particularly if the other clinic confirms it was him as well." The officer looked down at the paperwork in front of him. "However, it's a first offense and he's likely to be released on bail. It should be more than a slap on the wrist for sure, but it depends on how the judge views this."

"When will we know?"

"We should have more for you by the end of the day when you show up. But, if we don't by tonight, it could be a couple days. Depends on how quickly he's processed and bail set."

"Good enough." Zane stood and walked away; then he turned and looked back. "Does the dog have any rights?"

The cop looked at him, then slowly shook his head. "Not much."

"Pity," Zane said. "He's a vet too." Something he should look into more. Or at least have Badger ask Commander Cross about that. It hardly seemed fair. But that was like so much in life. Rarely was there justice for those that deserved it.

CHAPTER 8

THE END OF the day couldn't come fast enough for Holly. By the time she straightened from checking on the last surgery patient, her back was killing her, and her head was pounding. One of the surgeries had been delayed as the dog's owner hadn't followed the presurgery procedures. So no fixing the Lab's leg today. She moaned. "Done." She grinned at her assistant. "Thank heavens this last one went easy."

"You look like you're pretty tired," noted Beth, her surgical nurse, who came in just for surgery days.

"I am," Holly said with a brief smile. She glanced around. "But we did well today. Thank you for your help."

Beth gave her the same smile she always did. "You're more than welcome. You know that's why I'm here."

And Holly did know it. But she'd also seen a lot of assistants and surgical nurses who were here because of the paycheck, not because they cared. She considered herself blessed that Beth was one who cared.

Holly walked over to the sink and washed up, pulling off her mask and gown. With her arms scrubbed free of surgical leftovers, she turned back to see the small Chihuahua being moved into his cage. They'd have to watch him for the next couple hours, but, with any luck, he'd go home tonight. It hadn't been a major surgery, just a growth removed from the outside of the abdominal wall. Not that it wasn't always serious, but it could have been so much worse.

She checked his vitals once again. "Chico is doing well. Hopefully he can go home with his mom tonight."

"Maybe," Beth said, "but you know how I feel about that. Beside Katch is still here too."

"You can stay if you want," Holly said. "If Chico stays, you know one of us has to."

"I prefer to keep him overnight and to let him leave in the morning."

"Right," Holly said. "We'll check him in a couple hours and see how he's doing." She walked out, going to her office, brushing her hair off her forehead. She sat down, then realized she hadn't picked up a coffee. That was something she really needed.

Just then Mittle came in, bearing a hot cup for her. "I saw you go in without your coffee, so I figured I'd deliver."

"Oh, thank you." Grateful, Holly took the cup and sagged back in her chair, putting her feet up on her desk. "Long day," she said.

"No longer than most others," Mittle said. "But much worse because of not much sleep and the disruptions last night."

Holly nodded. "How is Katch doing?"

Mittle grinned. "I've been back and forth a couple times. I can't help it. Katch is very beautiful but looks like he's had a rough time."

"He has, indeed," Holly said. "After I have my coffee, I'll check on him. Just needed five minutes to recoup."

Mittle walked toward the door, calling back, "Take your time. I'll tell Zane that you'll be ready in a bit."

"Is Zane here?" she said, dropping her feet to the floor

and leaning forward in her chair. "If that's the case, send him in."

Mittle shot her a cheeky look. "Somehow that's what I figured you'd say." She disappeared out the door.

Holly groaned. The last thing she needed was her staff commenting on her love life. They had all been more than worried about her these last few years knowing what she'd been through. They had been instrumental in her making the effort to succeed here at her clinic. She took a sip of coffee as the door opened, letting in Zane. She smiled up at him. "How was your day?"

"Better than yours, apparently," he said, sitting across from her.

When he studied her face, she schooled her features so she wouldn't look quite so tired, but it was pretty darn hard when she was exhausted.

"Sounds like it's time to go home, grab some food and go to bed," he said. "Although we need to stop in at the station too."

"Right. I'd forgotten about that part," she said. "I have to check up on the patients, and I'll leave Beth here on watch. She'll call me if I'm needed."

"And Katch?"

She lifted her cup. "As soon as I'm done with this, I was going to check on him again. How did you do with the police?"

"Not very well," he said. "There are only a few laws against animal cruelty."

"I know," she said sadly. "We're always up against a very different mind-set when it comes to animals. We know there's a time when they need to be put down for their illness's sake and a time when we have to consider human safety over an animal's life, but I don't think either apply to this dog."

"Neither do I," he said. "So I'd like to get him as healthy as possible and find a better life for him."

"And how will you do that?"

He shook his head. "I haven't a clue."

"The dog could be happy here," she stated. "We just need to get the shooter to leave."

"That would be ideal," he said, "but Katch still doesn't have a home."

"You could keep him." She'd been uncertain about his reaction when mentioning this idea of hers, but he surprised her.

"I could," he said, "but, since I don't have a home or a safe place for him, that's hardly ideal. And I'm not sure it's a good idea for me to move back here either."

Her heart sank. She nodded but didn't say anything. She was too tired for this conversation, and she knew she couldn't hold back if it got truly personal. She had so much she needed to say, and yet, nothing would ever come out. So maybe the words didn't need to be said at all. She finished her coffee, pushed her chair back and, with an attempt at a bright smile, said, "I'm taking a look at him now."

He stood. "May I come?"

She considered the time, then nodded. "The girls should be done cleaning up after surgery." She led the way to the back to the surgical room.

Beth looked up and smiled. "Chico's doing fine."

"Good. How about Katch?"

Beth nodded. "Bettina has checked on him several times today. I updated the file, saying she upped the pain meds once, and then reduced them again when he seemed to be okay. I think he was just moving around in there and hurt himself."

"Has he been out?" Zane asked.

Beth nodded. "We took him out earlier, he's walking, but poorly. He needs to go out again." She checked the clock. "I'll do that when I'm done here."

"No need," Holly said, opening Katch's cage door. "I'll take him out right now. Zane can help."

Beth stood back and watched, but Holly could feel her curious gaze going from Zane to her. Holly introduced them and said, "Zane is my brother-in-law."

Carefully they helped Katch gain his feet and then walk, a strap under his belly to help carry some of his weight as they went outside to the back run. With Zane taking most of the dog's weight, they led him several times around the circle of the yard, giving him a chance to walk, to exercise the sore muscles, to smell some grass and fresh air and to finally lift his leg.

After he went to the bathroom twice, and, with Zane still mostly holding him up with the belly sling, Holly bent and checked over his face. "How you doing, boy?"

Katch just stood there and let her work on him.

"He seems to be very docile right now," Zane said.

"It's partly the medication he's getting." Holly checked his legs. They appeared to be scraped but were healing nicely. She searched on the side of his mouth where he had a bit of swelling. "Looks like he scratched the inside of his mouth too. But that's healing as well." She walked around the animal. "Can you ease up the sling? I want to see if he can support himself and for how long."

Zane slowly lowered the sling around the animal's belly. Katch stood tall and firm on his own. And then he tried to take a step or two, managed it, but he was weak and wobbly. Without the sling there to hold him, he would have fallen.

Holly nodded. "It's progress, just not enough. Let's get him back inside again."

They took him back and helped him into the cage. Immediately Katch collapsed far in the back of the cage and looked like he was snuggling in to sleep.

Holly changed out his food and water, made a notation on the chart and then straightened. "Beth, are you okay for the first two hours?"

"Might as well leave me here 'til midnight," she said. "You can relieve me then."

Holly walked back into the office. "I think I need food first. What about you?" She turned to Zane, who stood with a frown on his face. "What?"

"You have to come back at midnight?"

She nodded. "It's always like that when we have animals overnight. It's actually nice of Beth to stay 'til midnight. Otherwise, I'd be camping out here all night."

"And then what? You get up two or three times in the night to check on them?"

"Exactly," she said. "I set an alarm clock every four hours. If I'm more concerned, it's every two hours. And, if I'm really concerned, I don't go to sleep."

"Then why don't we stop at the police station first, then pick up some food, take it home, and see if you can get some sleep before your shift. I'll wake you up before midnight, and you can come down."

She smiled up at him. "That's not a bad idea. As long as I don't get a second wind, I might just crash for a few hours when we get home."

"Come on then."

He reached out a hand, and instinctively she put hers in it. As she stared down at his hand, she gave a head shake. *Remember, Holly. He's leaving. He's always left before, and this time is no different.*

HE WONDERED AT the look on her face when he grabbed her hand and led her out of the office. He knew they had an odd relationship, one that had taken a turn a few years back, and yet it, seemed to be coming back around again. He wasn't sure how he felt about it. And neither was he sure how he felt about moving back here. Now that thought tantalized him at the edges of his mind, making him consider if that was really what he was supposed to do. Not that Holly couldn't practice as a vet elsewhere, but he was the one without a home, while she had a home, her clinic, her staff …

It was almost like Badger had called it. Zane wanted to send him a text and tell him how he hated him for it, but, of course, that wasn't the truth. If this opened up to something beautiful, then maybe he owed Badger something extra for it. But it was hard to see anything in front of him right now. Things were a mess. Although he'd found Katch, they'd found the dog in very difficult circumstances, and it certainly wasn't an ideal start for the dog's new civilian life.

But Zane didn't know what he was supposed to do about it. This War Dogs assignment was up for interpretation, based on the individual handling each file. It wasn't like the government, Commander Cross or even Badger had given Zane strict parameters to work from. Hell, there were none at all. It was a case of check to make sure the dog was having a decent life. If not, then what? It seemed like Ethan had settled in with the dogs he had saved, turning it into a new business for him. Of course in Pierce's case, he'd reunited the dog to its owner. But, in this case, there didn't appear to be an owner. There'd been an adoptive family originally, but Katch never made it there. And that had been months ago. He'd likely been handed off to the wrong people over and over.

A part of Zane said Holly was the right person to take care of Katch, but could she handle the dog? It was one thing to deal with a large shepherd when it was sedated on your operating table or drugged in your clinic, but it was an entirely different thing to have a shepherd that big and wild and free in your backyard who didn't want to listen to your orders. And a one-hundred-pound woman walking a two-hundred-pound dog on a leash? Forget about it.

He sighed and stopped at his truck at the passenger's side. "I'll bring you back at midnight, so we might as well take the one vehicle home."

She shook her head. "No, I'll drive."

"You're too tired," he said, his voice stalwart.

She glared at him.

He grinned. "I know you want to be stubborn," he said, "but let's not take it too far." He watched as her shoulders sagged, and he could see the fatigue settling in deeper. He opened the truck door for her.

She nodded and hopped into the passenger side. He got in the driver's side and headed to the police station, where they were in and out in under thirty minutes. Outside the station he asked, "So is there any decent take-out food around here?"

"I'd prefer no pizza tonight," she said. "There is Indian

and Chinese and Greek."

"Objections to any of them?"

"No, I just object to having to choose." She smothered a yawn. "You're right. I'm tired."

"Decision made then," he said. "Indian. Where is it?"

She gave him directions, and soon he pulled up out front. He walked into the restaurant, leaving her with her head leaning back, her eyes closed in the front of his truck.

Inside, at the cashier, he asked, "What's fast and ready to go?"

"Butter chicken is ready. Roti is ready. We have a few other items here." He pointed at the front, where there was a large glass case. "And then everything on the menu won't take too long to get ready, maybe ten to fifteen minutes."

He considered his time frame. "Let's just get butter chicken for two, roti, and some of those vegetables and pakoras." As the man started to dish it up, Zane changed his mind. "Actually make it enough for four people."

Before long the order sat on the counter. Zane paid for it, picked up the bag, nodded his thanks and headed out to the truck. He hopped in and asked in a low voice, "You awake?"

"I am," she whispered. "But only just."

"We'll be home in five," he said, "then dinner, and afterward you can crash."

She gave a light sigh, opened her eyes and smiled up at him. It was the same smile she used to give him that made him feel like he was the most special person in the whole world, how he felt so damn lucky because she would look at him that way. He hadn't ever had anybody else give him anything close to that look.

He turned on the truck, backed out of the parking lot

and headed to her place, his mind in a turmoil, trying to figure out what the hell he was supposed to do at this stage of his life.

"Did I do something wrong?" she asked, her voice hesitant.

He shot her a quick glance of surprise. "No, of course not. Why?"

"You suddenly withdrew," she said, "as if you were uncomfortable or upset about something."

"The butter chicken is going cold," he said with a half laugh. "No, I'm just fine." He reached over and squeezed her fingers.

She caught his fingers in hers and just hung on.

He knew they were heading down a path, ... but they both had to be sure they wanted to go there.

CHAPTER 9

"**H**OLLY?" A GENTLE murmur broke through her dream state. Her eyes flew open, and she stared up at Zane. She reached up. "You're home?" She had a quiet joy in her voice.

He frowned at her and sat beside her, his weight shifting her body. "I've been here all evening," he said gently. "Time to wake up. You have to go to the clinic to relieve Beth from her shift."

Holly blinked up at him several times as she tried to remove the cobwebs to understand what he said. Finally it filtered back in. She groaned. "Wow. I didn't know if I was dreaming. It was so lifelike, but from years ago, when once again you were gone and then suddenly came home again."

"It's probably not all that far off to the reality of what you're experiencing right now," he admitted. "But I'm no longer in the navy."

"No," she said sadly. "But you'll still leave." On that note, she got up and made her way to the bathroom, closing the door. She washed her face, used the toilet and, by the time she was done, she felt a whole lot more awake. She stepped out and said, "I feel like I almost got a full night's sleep."

"It's eleven-thirty," he said. "So you got a good five hours, if not a little bit more. You only ate a little before you crashed. How hungry are you now?"

"I'm not," she said, "but I might take some with me. I'll be awake for the first hour for sure, and then I might sleep after that. Beth hasn't called, I presume, so I gather everything is okay at the clinic?" She checked her phone and nodded. "No messages, so we'll take that as a good sign."

"Good," he said. "Let's get something packed to go then." He turned and walked out of her bedroom, going to the kitchen.

She followed him and watched as he packed up the take-out containers. "We don't have to take it all."

"Might as well," he said. "There isn't all that much left anyway." He shrugged. "I'm a big eater, and you need to eat more."

On that note, she had a suspicion in the back of her mind forming. "Are you planning on staying at the clinic tonight too?" She worked hard to keep her tone neutral but figured she'd failed completely when he looked back at her and nodded.

"Absolutely," he said. "Especially when you're alone."

That made her worry about Beth. "Do you think that's why she hasn't contacted me?" She chewed her bottom lip. "I don't even think I warned her."

"Let's go see," he said.

Within minutes they were in his vehicle headed to the clinic.

No lights were on, and that was normal. It didn't look like there'd been a break-in, but it was too early to tell.

Holly hopped out and headed for the front door, shut off the alarm before it could go off, relieved to see it was still set. She walked through to the back office to find Beth sleeping soundly. Holly walked over, tapped her assistant on the shoulder.

Beth's eyes opened, and she hopped to her feet. "Oh, my God! I fell asleep," she said, rubbing her face. "Sorry about that. I didn't think I would need to. But then, all of a sudden, I went to lay down just to rest a little bit." She had a wry smile. "And I guess I was out almost instantly."

"How are the patients?"

"Last I checked, they were both fine," she said, leading the way to the cages.

Chico looked up, and his tail wagged as they approached him.

"He's looking pretty good."

They both checked his tubes and his medication levels, gave him a bit of a cuddle, and then Holly turned to look at Katch. He was awake and watching them from inside with an alertness to him that hadn't been there earlier.

Holly crouched in front of his unlocked cage, which was normal for these overnight cases, so they could access the patient faster. "How are you doing, Katch?"

At the sound of his name, his ears tweaked. But now Katch's alertness gave Holly an uneasy sensation. Katch appeared to be staring at Zane.

She looked over at him and said, "I don't know if he's comfortable with you right now or not or if something else is bothering him."

Zane crouched in front of Katch and talked to him in a gentle tone. He seemed to relax slightly, but his gaze kept going to the entrance of the cage between the two of them. Zane stood. "Don't take him out without me here." He turned and headed back to the front of the office.

She knew he would check around the grounds and was grateful for his presence.

Beth put on her coat. "You okay if I leave now?"

Holly locked Katch's cage and stood, giving her assistant a hug. "Absolutely." She walked her to the front door. Zane was there. She asked him, "Can you walk Beth out to the car please?"

"Absolutely not," Beth said. "No fussing."

"No arguing," Holly said firmly. "Zane is here, and it won't take him more than a couple minutes."

She stood at the front door, waiting as Zane walked Beth to her car and stood by as she got in, turned on the engine and headed out.

When Zane returned, Holly reset the alarm. "I didn't reset it when we first came in," she said in a low voice.

Zane nodded. "I noticed. I did a check, but I'd like to do another one."

"And we need to take the animals outside."

They headed into the back again. Almost immediately she heard Katch's subtle low growl.

Zane whispered, "Shit." He turned to her. "You stick with me. Obviously we've got a problem."

"You think the intruder is here?"

"No idea what's going on, but, from Katch's point of view, there is an immediate threat."

Hating to even think such a thing, Holly followed Zane from room to room, closet to closet, as he searched, while she stood in the hallway, making sure nobody changed areas while he was doing one.

When they came back to Katch's room, the dog was still alert and tense, the ridge on the back of his neck thick and angry-looking.

"What if he's just sensing him, like maybe he's outside?" Holly pointed to the windows. "Maybe he saw him through the window."

"It's possible," Zane said. "The good thing is, he's not inside right now. Which is where we don't want him."

"So do we need to check outside?" she asked nervously.

"We need to," he said.

"Honestly, I'm not too sure I want to. He had a gun. He didn't shoot us last time, but, if we stand between him and the dog, who knows how determined he is to make sure Katch dies?"

"I want you to stay locked up inside, so I don't have to worry about you."

She frowned. "And what if he comes back inside?"

"The alarm will go off, and I'll hear it," he said. "And I'll be inside in a heartbeat. More than that, I want you to stay here with Katch. Let him know you're not the bad guy, and you're here for him."

"More than likely he'll think I'm hiding out with Chico, not him," she said with a laugh. And Katch wouldn't be far wrong.

"It doesn't matter what Katch thinks," Zane said. "The problem is, he's giving us signals, and we need to listen."

She couldn't argue with that. "I'll put on coffee. Maybe warm up some food," she said, as if distracting herself.

He grinned. "Do that. I ate most of it already when you were sleeping." And, on that note, he disappeared out the back.

She swore softly but walked into the staff room, put on coffee, dished up a portion of food and put it in the microwave. She kept looking from window to window, wondering what the hell was going on outside. When her food was heated, and the coffee was ready, she walked back in to where the cages were and sat down on the floor beside the two dogs.

"I'm not doing this to torment you," she said to Katch. "Honestly, you shouldn't be eating human food anyway. And, if you're hungry, you have dog food in your cage."

But Katch was definitely interested in her late-night dinner. She sighed, feeling guilty. She got up and walked over to the cupboard and pulled out a couple small beef jerky sticks for the dog. She gave him one through the cage opening. After sniffing it delicately, Katch took it between his teeth and dropped it, then chewed on it, eating it slowly.

"Well, that's as nice a manner as I've ever seen a dog eat a treat," she commented. "And, unlike you, I'm going to eat this as I normally do." She attacked her food with a hungry vengeance.

She felt quite decent, considering how much sleep she'd had. Too bad it was the middle of the night right now. Somehow she had to wear off some of this energy, then crash again so she could function in the morning. If she didn't sleep more soon, her morning schedule would be brutal again, and the cycle would just continue.

With her own food gone, and the second treat in Chico's mouth, the three of them sat here quietly while Holly sipped her coffee. She needed Zane to come back so they could take the dogs outside. But she wouldn't go out there as long as Zane was doing his protector thing because she had no doubt it would interfere with whatever plan he had.

She wondered what he did in the navy where this was the work he instinctively knew how to handle. And what could he possibly do now that he was out of the military and living supposedly a normal life with his rare and dangerous skill set? What kind of a company was Titanium Corp? He'd said something about security, but was that like being a bodyguard? Or was that like being a security guard, over-night at an empty station to make sure hoodlums didn't get into the building? Surely there was work like that for him here. But she highly doubted that was what he wanted to do. Then again, she had no clue what he wanted to do. He had only just now revealed to her that all he'd ever wanted was to be in the navy.

And then she realized how hard that must have been for him when he had to leave the navy. All she'd ever wanted was to be a vet, and she was currently working her dream job. But, if she didn't do this, what else would she do? She couldn't think of anything else that she would want to do as much. Except maybe be a mom. But that didn't have to be a case of one or the other. She could certainly do both at the same time. What about him? He was out of the navy and somehow on a trip across the country to retrieve a dog. No, not even retrieve—more like a welfare check.

She looked down at Katch. "You must be something special." Her gentle murmur caused Katch's ears to twitch, and those huge brown eyes looked up at her. "You actually have his full attention. I don't. I'm just a side thought. And I bet, if he'd had the chance to go anywhere but Maine, he would have. But he's here now. The question is, how do we both manage to keep him? Because I think he's your answer. It will take somebody like him to handle you."

She didn't think Zane had had a lot of dog training, but he certainly had a way with animals; that she knew. She'd watched deer walk right up and smell his hands. She'd watched squirrels hop onto his fingers and run up his arms to sit on his shoulder. No doubt he was gifted, but what did one do with gifts like that when it came to finding a way to make a living? And had the Titanium Corp paid his way here? Not to mention the dog's vet bills? It made the most sense but she hadn't actually asked him.

There were so many unanswered questions that it made her curious about the life he had lived in the navy, curious about the life he could see himself living now. There'd been absolutely no contact, as far as she knew, with his father or brother since he'd arrived that first night. Sure, only a couple nights has passed, but, if it were her brother, though she didn't have any, but, if it were her brother, she would have definitely contacted him on a daily basis. But it seemed like these men just didn't want anything to do with each other.

Brody had been the more genial and jovial of the lot. But even he hadn't had much to do with his father and brothers. Brody dealt with his father because his father didn't seem to deal with anybody else, but Brody hadn't particularly liked it. He used to say the old man was too dependent on him. *What would Dad do if something happened to me?* She admonished herself for not realizing just how prophetic Brody's words had been, and, as far as his father was concerned, he was basically drinking himself to death.

Given that thought, Butch came to mind. He didn't seem to care about anything. Hopefully he cared about Sandra.

What was there for Zane here? Not his birth family it seemed. She could hope it was her. She did have her own house at this point. So she was certainly okay as long as she kept her practice, and she didn't really feel the need to move anywhere. But, if Zane asked her to, would she?

She winced at that, because, of course, how could she ask him to pull up whatever life he had built to come back to a place he didn't want to be if she wasn't prepared to do the same, to move to a new location with him?

"Oh, the twisted lives we lead," she said to Katch. "You're in the same boat, aren't you? Nobody to love you, looking for a home, not too sure this is where you belong, because look what has happened to you."

She looked out the window again and said, "What are you doing, Zane? Hurry up, please."

ZANE SHIFTED THROUGH the darkness, keeping the clinic in sight, and listened to the night. He'd had way-too-much experience hunting. Both animal and people. He had a skill for it, mostly because the animals would let him walk past them in the woods and never give any warning. Here he had no weapons. And that put him at a disadvantage. He didn't know what had triggered Katch's response, but Zane wouldn't ignore it.

John McAfee should have been held behind bars, but Zane suspected the police had let McAfee out on bail, which would mean he'd come right back here again. Zane couldn't get much information out of the police on the matter either. Maybe they knew he wouldn't like what they had to say.

Until McAfee did something serious. Obviously breaking and entering into two vet clinics probably wasn't considered bad enough to keep him in jail. Or he'd escaped. Would the cops have even let him and Holly know that McAfee was on the lose?

He pulled out the cop's card and sent a text, not expecting a response, given the time of night—or early morning now technically. Instead, he got a reply fairly quickly.

He was released. He's to show up in court in two weeks.

"Dammit," Zane said, swearing under his breath. That was no help. **Wish you had told us,** he texted. **I'm standing guard outside the vet clinic right now because we think somebody's here.**

The response came back, **Think?**

Think. The dog is reacting like he's in danger. And I don't trust that asshole intruder one bit.

There was no response for a long moment, and then the officer sent another text. **I'm here, working late. If you want, I can drive past and take a look.**

I'm already here, and the dog is inside, he typed. **But, if you drive past, it might help McAfee realize you are keeping an eye on the place.**

Will do, he replied.

Zane put away his phone and shifted his position, looking for any signs of McAfee. But there hadn't been anything, not a branch breaking, nothing. If this guy had been overseas in the military, he was likely as good as, if not better trained, than Zane was.

He waited in the darkness. It took only about ten minutes before a car's headlights came down the street toward him. This area was relatively quiet at night, so this was the first car since Zane had come outside. It swung into the parking lot, and, sure enough, it was a cop car. The guy got out, reached in, grabbed his flashlight and walked around the clinic.

Zane texted Holly to say a cop was doing a search and to stay inside. When he got her **Okay** response, he felt better. His eyes moving slowly, he watched to see if anybody else was out here who wasn't so happy about the cop's presence. Somebody who might take this opportunity to disappear. Zane thought he saw a shadow about thirty feet to the right of the clinic, which would put him directly on the far side of where Zane currently was, which was crappy positioning. He judged the distances around, wondering where the shadow was moving to, and saw it creep around farther in the back of the property.

Zane headed for a meet-up with somebody skulking in the dark.

CHAPTER 10

GETTING THAT TEXT had been both good and bad. It had roused Holly from nodding off as she curled up against the cages, not willing to leave Katch or Chico. And it had easily explained the flashlight she could see, now that she was awake. It had alerted her that Zane was fine and still on the lookout. But it also reminded her of the dangers out there ...

She wanted to text him again and ask when he was coming back inside but knew that was probably not a good idea. If he didn't have his phone on Airplane mode, and he was creeping up on somebody, then that would give away his position. And how rotten that she had to even consider such a thing.

Finally she had to get up to move around; her legs were so stiff. She couldn't see anything or anyone. The cop car was parked in front, for which she was grateful. But she suspected everything was happening on the back end of the clinic, where she had very little view.

The main rear door led out to the back fenced-in area, but she dared not open it. It was attached to the security alarm, so hopefully the intruder wouldn't easily gain access that way with his second attempt here at Katch. She needed to reconsider the security coverage here too, adding security sensors to all back doors. Hopefully the other vets wouldn't put up a fight about it. Although they were doing okay here together, they weren't making great money in the clinic, not to handle every new expense, but it was a living.

At that word she winced. That was really crappy vocabulary for her to use.

With the cop outside with Zane, Holly walked around the clinic several more times and grabbed her laptop, moving back into the rear room with the dogs. There she caught up on some of her reports, fired off a bunch of emails that needed to be done and then surfed the web. Anything to keep her mind off what was going on outside.

When she heard an odd sound at the back door, she froze. She shut down her laptop, placed it on the counter in front of her and slid to her feet. She checked out Katch's position, but he was calm, relaxed.

"Does that mean it's Zane?" she asked.

Katch just looked at her steadily.

She could almost see it in his eyes. *Why are you asking me?*

Holly hated to admit it, but the dogs were much better at sorting out predators from prey. Humans sucked at it. She waited a few more minutes to see if she heard any more sounds. When she didn't, she slipped around to the back door and peered out through the blinds. She made sure she just lifted a corner and didn't bend it. But she saw nothing out there. There was nothing in the pen, nothing at all out back.

Frustrated she turned around. Through the hallway she could see the cop standing at her front glass doors, talking on his radio. She wanted to race out and talk to him, but again she was thinking of Zane. She pulled out her phone and decided to send him a text. **Is the cop leaving?**

Maybe, came back the reply. **Stay inside. McAfee's here.**

Her heart froze at that. What had been a possibility was now an actual fact. And that was the last thing she wanted. She raced back to sit down between the two dogs. She looked over at Chico. "We should've sent you home last night, shouldn't we have?"

He whined.

She reached several fingers through the cage and gently stroked his head. She didn't want to bring him out because of the tubes. Nor did she want that asshole coming in here and trying to shoot more than just one dog. Neither of these animals deserved to be shot. But somebody was hell-bent on taking out Katch for sure.

Just then she heard a vehicle start up and pull away. She laid her head back and groaned. "If that's the cop leaving, you can bet we're about to see some action," she muttered. She pulled her knees up to her chest, wrapped her arms around them tight and dropped her head on them.

In the darkness she sat, waiting.

THE COP HAD texted Zane several times, saying he couldn't see anyone. Zane had replied, **He's here. The shadow just moved around back.**

I'm not going after him without backup, the cop texted. **I'll pull the vehicle around to the back of the next block and walk over.**

And with that, Zane moved around into a better position to see where the shadow was. As the cop took off, it was like the shadow froze, then crept a little closer to the clinic.

But unfortunately the cop made it obvious by going around one corner and then another corner and parking. Zane just stared in shock. "Like that'll do anything," he muttered silently.

And, of course, the intruder would know that too. Which was the worst thing that could happen.

Just then the shadow melted back again into the distance. Zane took several more steps in that direction. He really needed McAfee to do something, so Zane could take him down, take him out. Because skulking around on the property would only get McAfee a trespassing charge. And maybe a court order to stay away. But that was all. And both were worthless as far as protecting Katch from McAfee.

As the cop walked back around, he whistled. Zane realized the cop really didn't think anything was wrong. But then again, it was *just a dog*. Who gave a shit, right? As the cop came around, he suddenly stopped, pivoted and called out, "Hey, who's there?"

And then McAfee did something Zane had never expected but changed the game entirely.

McAfee pulled the trigger.

The cop went down with a roar, crying out as he hit the sidewalk hard. And then the shadow blended into the darkness.

Zane was torn. He wanted to go after that asshole, but he didn't dare leave the cop to bleed out on the sidewalk. It might already be too late to save the policeman, but, as a tactic, it was a hell of a nice move. It was intended to flush Zane out of the shadows, and it would do that. But he couldn't afford to take a bullet himself.

He texted Holly to call 9-1-1, that a cop was down. And reminded her to stay inside. He didn't get a response back, so he hoped to hell she'd done it.

His phone buzzed a minute later with **Done**. She followed up with **Can you help him?**

Intruder is still here, he typed. **The second bullet's got my name on it.**

Stay there, stay there, her text came back urgently. **Cops are on the way.**

He could hear sirens in the distance, and then a rustle of brushes as the intruder took off.

Knowing he had no choice, Zane ran alongside the back of the clinic, around to where the cop was. Zane knelt at the man's side. "Take it easy," he said, "we've got an ambulance on the way."

The cop opened his eyes. "I didn't think it was serious," he gasped, his hand over his shoulder, blood oozing through his fingers. "I just figured he was some asshole coming back after more drugs."

"Oh, he's an asshole all right," Zane said, ripping the cop's shirt open so he could see the damage. He placed his hand over the wound. "The trouble is, he's just seriously upped his game."

With Zane's other hand, he pulled out his phone and called Holly. "Can you bring some gauze and something to put pressure on the officer's shoulder? The cops are on the way, but he's bleeding pretty badly."

The door at the back of the clinic burst open, and she ran out.

He grabbed the gauze and said, "Get back inside. Make sure he doesn't circle around, find another way in."

With a shocked look, she turned and bolted back inside again.

"You're really trying to protect that dog?" the cop said.

"Why do you care?"

"Because he did a lot to serve our country," Zane answered quietly. "So did I. And it feels like we've both been abandoned."

The cop looked up, and understanding whispered across his face. "I guess I can see that. You could always go into law enforcement. God knows we need good men."

Zane chuckled. "I don't know that I'm cut out for that. You take them off the street, and the judge releases them. What the hell are you supposed to do with that?"

"True enough." He winced. "How bad is it?" he asked abruptly.

"It's high in the shoulder. You'll survive," Zane said, "but you really should be still, just so you don't bleed out too much before we get you some medical care."

The cop just smiled. "I'm getting married next month," he said. "I would like to make that date."

"We'll ensure that you do," Zane said. "But now we have a bigger problem as this asshole has blood in his eyes. I don't know what triggered it tonight, but he seemed to think you were a threat in some way."

"I'm not sure he thought I was a threat as much as he thought I was just debris in his way. He had a very cocky attitude at the station. As in a *seriously you can't touch me* type of a thing. He pissed us off with that. But then we found out he was allowed to leave. According to his lawyer, he hadn't done anything. McAfee changed his story several times, using the excuse he was afraid the cops would treat him badly, so he lied. Like we give a damn about beating up these jerks," he said. "We just want to take the assholes off the street, but the assholes are getting away with everything these days."

"Maybe," Zane said. "But, in this case, he's not going to

get away with attempted murder of a police officer. That's guaranteed jail time. So possible suicide by cop? Or maybe just a man out of control. But still had to have something set him off."

"Maybe but I have no idea what." The cop looked up at him. "If you don't mind, I'd like to pass out now."

Zane nodded. "You do that. You'll be in the hospital in no time."

In the background he could hear the sirens getting louder, closer. But he was also concerned about another bullet coming his way. He didn't dare move the cop, so he stayed low to the ground.

As soon as the ambulance pulled up, and the cops appeared, Zane cried out, pointing in the direction the gunman had gone. "He's taken off in that direction. I'm not even sure we're safe here."

The cops fanned out and took off.

The paramedics came to his side.

"He's got one bullet high in the shoulder," Zane said. "He's bleeding pretty badly. But I don't think it's fatal."

"Step back and let us take a look," one of the paramedics said as they both dropped to the ground to run a check on the policeman's vitals.

Zane knew he wasn't needed here anymore, and he sure as hell didn't dare go out searching for this guy with the cops out there because Zane could be taken for the wrong man. So his best position right now was to go back to Holly and to stand by her side.

As the injured cop was loaded into the ambulance, he called out, "Zane?"

Zane, halfway to the clinic, stepped around to the end of the ambulance. "Yeah, I'm here."

The guy looked up at him and said, "Thanks."

"Don't thank me," Zane said. "It's because of me that you got shot."

"No," he said. "It was the system that let this asshole back out on the streets. But I'm still alive, and, for that, you get my thanks."

With a nod, Zane headed into the clinic. As he opened the door, he knew the alarm would go off. He headed in anyway.

Holly stood at the entrance and shut off the alarm. As soon as he was inside, she turned it back on again, then threw herself into his arms. "Oh, my God," she said. "He actually shot a cop?"

He held her tight. "Yes, he did. And that changes the game entirely."

"I know." She leaned back to look up at his face, reached up with both hands on his cheeks. "You realize you're next."

Grimly, he looked down at her and nodded. "Not just me though," he said. "You too. You're the one who saved Katch."

She frowned and shook her head. "No, I don't think he'd blame me. I think it's more a case of transference to you. You're the one blocking his move every time."

"Maybe," he admitted because there was a certain amount of sense to that. "But that doesn't mean he won't transfer it again to whoever it is keeping Katch alive."

She nodded. "That's possible. But I can't worry about that. Do you think it's safe to take the dogs out now?"

He nodded. "A lot of cops are around. I doubt McAfee's anywhere within the vicinity. We'll stay close to the building and the fences."

They took little Chico out, so he could do his business,

and took him right back in again. Then they brought Katch out. He moved stiffly, his ears up, aware and weary.

"Do you think it's safe?" she muttered from the doorway.

"I do," he said. "But we'll let Katch tell us."

They let him out to do his business and to walk for a moment. He wasted no time emptying his bladder, then his bowels. And almost immediately the hair on the back of his neck went up.

Zane turned to Holly. "Get back inside now."

She looked at him, startled, then bolted inside.

He nudged Katch along, but he needed no urging either. Within seconds, they were back inside. Once there, Zane turned and stared out through the open doorway. "I know he's out there, Katch. We'll get him. I promise."

Katch shot him a look as if to say, *Yeah, right.*

Zane reached down and scratched Katch under the chin and head, then shut the door in front of him. "Honest," he said.

A hard *ping* hit the exterior door. He stared at it and shook his head. "See? He didn't even try that time. It's obvious the door was closed, so that was just a shot in frustration."

Holly bolted toward him. "Oh, my God! Did he just shoot the door?"

"Yes, he did," Zane said. "But I think more because he couldn't get into position to get a decent shot."

"So he is still out there," she cried out in fear. "What's to stop him from coming back tomorrow or the next day?"

"I don't know," he said honestly. "Hopefully the cops will stop him, now that they're motivated because this guy shot one of their own."

"But they're out there looking," she cried out. "And yet, McAfee shot right into the door."

"True," he said, "which is why I need you to stay inside. Although I wasn't planning on going back outside, now I think I have to."

She shook her head. "No, no, no, no. The cops will shoot you. He'll shoot you. You need to stay here with me."

He looked at her for a long moment and then smiled. "You don't want me to stay to keep you safe. You want me to stay so I stay safe."

"Of course," she said. "I don't want to lose you. Not again."

Prophetic words. He looked at her in surprise.

She nodded. "You must know that I've always loved you."

He shook his head. "And yet, you married my brother."

"Yes," she said in frustration. "I did. And I loved him too. But I only came to love him because I knew you were gone, that you weren't ever coming back."

He frowned. "We were already broken up. You were free to be with my brother." He stared off, confused and angry at the emotions tumbling through him.

"We've been over this," she said. "All of that is true, but that doesn't mean I don't care. That I didn't love you first. That I'm *in love with you*. Always have been."

That caused Zane to pause, taking it all in.

"Even when mad at you. Even while I've waited for you to return since."

He winced at that. "That was the big thing with you. You hated the fact you always had to wait for me to come home."

"Yes," she said, "it was a big deal. But I've also grown

up. And I know that sometimes this is life. And, if I want to have a life with you, then this is the life I would have."

"Except I'm not in the military anymore," he said harshly. "I'm hardly a decent veteran. I have a pension, money for retraining and some savings but I don't even have a damn job. At least not a permanent one."

She took a deep breath, as if trying to hold back some of her own emotions. "I understand that, but I also know you'll figure it out. You were always very capable in figuring life out. However, if you go out there right now and get shot, you won't get time to figure anything out. We won't get time to figure *us* out."

At that, he looked down at her, and she reached up and kissed him. But not a gentle, easy kiss. It was a kiss of longing and urging and pain. And it was the pain that got to him. He wrapped her up tight in his arms and crushed her against his chest and kissed her back with a fervor that surprised him—and maybe her too.

When he finally lifted his head, she looked up at him, a smoky passion in her eyes, and she said, "See? We're still there underneath all this talk, underneath all these years and underneath all this emotion and whatever it was that went awry. It's still there. It's still us. We are still together. Whether you're ready to admit it or not."

"I know," he said gently. "I just don't know what to do about it."

"We need time," she said. "If you go out there, we won't have that time."

"I can't spend my life hiding." He stepped back, putting her firmly to the side. "That doesn't work. And, if I go out there, it won't be with the intention of not coming back."

"He's got a gun. You don't," she cried out. "If he gets a

chance, he'll shoot you."

"He has to get that opportunity first," Zane said firmly. "And I'm no slouch when it comes to defensive measures. Believe me. He won't get that chance."

And he turned and walked back out into the dark night.

CHAPTER 11

HOLLY RETURNED TO her office and lay down on the cot. It was damn-near impossible to calm down with Zane outside. The last time he'd gone out there, a cop had been shot. What were the chances he would come back unscathed?

She hated to admit how much she loved him and how much just seeing him again hurt her. She was an adult now, a seasoned adult who certainly wasn't the same as when he went back to the military, each and every time when he was on leave.

But it felt like she was losing him all over again. If he left again, there was a good chance it was final. Did he even consider what that was like for her? Chances were he didn't.

How could she not make the comparison? McAfee was a dangerous man. He'd had no problem shooting that poor cop. He'd gone from trying to kill a dog to trying to kill a police officer. That was one hell of a jump, and he'd barely hesitated. The fact that Zane was out there hunting him—and Zane was unarmed—just made the situation so much more intolerable.

As she lay here in the darkness, every sound was magnified—a bird, a stone being kicked, the breeze through the trees, a vehicle down the road. Everything made her back tingle with a thousand nerve endings. Twice she jolted up at sounds she was sure came from inside. And each time it was nothing. There would be no sleep for her for the rest of this night. She wanted to get up and put on coffee, maybe do some work, but she didn't know if she could do it in the dark.

Then she realized just enough light was inside the building that she could see quite easily. Which meant it had to be lightening up outside too.

She walked into the staff room, put on yet another pot of coffee, and then headed in to check on the dogs. Chico lay curled up in a tiny ball, his eyes huge. But Katch sat, as much as he could in his cage, his eyes, ears, the nape of his neck, all at attention. Hating to see the dog so wary and so aware, magnifying her own feelings of danger, Holly bent and gently stroked the dog's nose as much as she could through the cage.

"I'm sorry, sweetie. I don't know what's going on out there."

She knew the dog had absolutely no chance if the guy came inside. He was completely cornered and couldn't fight back. And that gave her another idea.

Or would it be foolish to let the dog out? It would be good for him to walk around a little bit, see how strong he was, but she might also have a hell of a time getting him to go back in the cage. But, then again, if he was strong enough to walk around the clinic on his own, maybe he didn't need to stay here. Maybe he could go home to somebody. The problem was, *what* somebody? Where would Katch go?

She stood, walked back to the coffeepot and poured herself a cup. Then in the hallway between the cages and the offices and the reception area, she leaned against the wall and contemplated her options.

If Katch could get out of the cage, what would he do? Would he race to a door and start howling and growling at something outside? Because that would make it even more intolerable in here. Would he hide, terrified of what was coming? In that case, Holly knew she would hide right beside him. She could be brave in certain circumstances, but this was not her forte. She wanted to be home, safe and sound, thinking about sunshine and roses, not predators in the night and especially not men who would shoot a dog without a care and then shoot a cop because he was in the way.

Something was so completely wrong about that scenario.

She sipped her coffee and waited for word from Zane. And still there was nothing and more nothing.

She thought the cops would come back or that more cops would come. She thought something would have happened by now. She checked her watch and realized over an hour and a half had passed since the cops had arrived en masse. Why wasn't a cop at the cruisers in her parking lot, running a command center or some such thing? Why had they all gone out into the woods? And, if they were all out there, how had the guy with the gun still shot at her back door? Had he taken out all the cops?

Her heart sank as she thought about it. Those men didn't deserve that. And she'd feel forever guilty if McAfee had done that.

Then she had another thought. An even worse thought. *If all the cops were out there, what's stopping the gunman from being right here at the clinic?*

She slowly slid down until she squatted at the base of the wall in the hallway. She was frozen. She had to think. *Think, Holly!*

She heard a doorknob, or she thought it was a doorknob. She peered forward to the front doors, but they were both locked, and there was no sign of anybody through the glass. She headed to the treatment room, but it was locked too. The back door was locked. So had somebody tried and given up?

Her phone buzzed in her hand. She pulled it out to see a message from Zane. **He's approaching the clinic.**

"Shit, shit, shit," she whispered.

She raced back into the room where the dogs were. She didn't quite close the door to this room, leaving it slightly ajar, and waited. Surely the security system would go off. The only good thing was the fact that Zane knew, so he couldn't be far away. Hopefully he'd marshaled some of the cops as well. Because, sure as hell, somebody needed to give them a hand right now. This was past ridiculous.

She crouched on the floor beside Katch, who was showing his teeth as she stared at the doorway. If that guy made it inside the door, they would both get shot. She just knew it.

She unlocked the gate and opened Katch's cage. Grabbing his collar, she led him out gently, moving both of them under a table, so they weren't in the direct line of sight once the door was open. The dog sat at her side, his lips curled, but he never made a sound. His ears were pointed forward, and his body was tense. He seemed to completely ignore his injuries. His eyes were focused on whatever was happening on the other side of that door.

Holly wrapped an arm around his chest and whispered against his ear, "Gentle, boy. Take it easy."

Katch appeared to calm. He certainly wasn't objecting to Holly's touch. Maybe he knew Holly was one of those who had worked so hard to patch him up.

And then she heard one of the exterior doors open. She waited, counting in her head ten seconds until the alarm went off. When she crossed the fifteen-second mark, she knew she was in deep shit because somebody had somehow disabled her security system. She looked over at Chico, who was now curled up at the far back end of his cage, terrified.

Instead of being terrified, Katch's muscles were rigid. He looked ready to spring forward. They were still under the table. Katch might lean forward, easily stepping out from under here, but it would be hard for Holly to get out quickly.

Then she heard one footstep in the hallway and another one. She shuddered and closed her eyes. Holding the dog tight, she kept whispering, "Easy. Take it easy."

In her mind she figured Zane was racing toward them, somehow saving them at the last moment. When she didn't hear any other footsteps, she realized Zane was probably still on his way here. Of course he was on his way. He'd given her full warning. But, for whatever reason, he hadn't quite made it here yet. She didn't dare think about all the reasons why.

And then the door to this room was pushed open. From under the table she could see the gunman's feet—heavy work boots and khakis. Of course he had khakis, hunter's khakis, and, from where she sat, she could see the long rifle tip as he had it pointed downward. He studied the room, and she realized, her heart sinking, that she'd left the dog's cage open.

The man swore gently. "Damn bitch took the dog."

She froze at the sound of his voice. She didn't recognize it, thank God, but it was enough to send jitters down her back. The dog was straining at her restraint. She couldn't tell if it was in terror or in anger.

And then she heard another footstep. She watched those feet suddenly back up, the rifle coming up, pointing down the hallway. And she realized Zane could be coming in the back door, coming into a trap, to face a killer.

She released the dog, grabbed a knife off her surgical tray, and, as Katch bounded toward the intruder, his mouth open, teeth bared, a growl coming from the back of his throat, she raced toward the intruder herself, a scalpel in hand, ready to stab him.

The man turned, startled by the attack. He pulled his rifle up and tried to turn, but he couldn't get the rifle down again to shoot the dog in such close quarters.

Katch grabbed his shoulder and bit down hard. McAfee roared, swearing in a frenetic manner as he fought off the dog, trying to beat him back.

She knew Katch was injured, knew Katch couldn't do much, yet she couldn't get close enough to get around the dog to stab the intruder. She slashed out at his hand, anything that was skin: his face, his neck, trying to get him to stop hurting the dog. The man kept hollering.

And suddenly Zane was here.

The fighting was a crazy melee of sounds, explosions and movements. And then it was over. She heard more sounds of running footsteps and the dog whimpering in her arms.

She bent closer to cuddle Katch, seeing broken stitches and further bleeding. She peered around the doorway to see Zane struggling to his feet and bolting after the gunman. At least his rifle had been left behind. She stared at it with revulsion. That was the last thing she wanted, but at least that meant the asshole didn't have it. Although somebody like McAfee probably had more than one.

She took a careful look at the dog's shoulder and added

some antibiotic ointment, cleaned it and put fresh gauze on top of it. The dog just lay here, whimpering. "I'm so sorry he hurt you again."

But the dog had fought, and the dog had won, at least at this point.

She administered some pain medicine and knew the chances of getting the dog to go back in the cage were pretty slim, but she thought she'd try. She opened the cage door wide, put a clean blanket in and called him over. "Come on, boy. Go in and lie down. I'll check on you in a little bit again."

Katch looked at her and slowly made his way inside the cage, curling up in the far back.

Holly stroked his forehead until he fell asleep. She wrote a note on the dog's chart, then got up. She put a call into 9-1-1 and explained what had happened. Once she said at least a half-dozen cops were out here, and she was worried about their health, the dispatcher got alarmed and said she was sending men out immediately. She warned Holly to not touch the weapon.

She stared down at it and said, "I have no wish to touch the gun, so the sooner you get somebody here, the better. If that guy circles around and comes back inside for it, I don't even want to contemplate …"

"Don't touch it. Stay on the line. I've got men coming."

"I don't want to stay on the line," she cried out. "I need to sit down." When she realized she was talking on her cell phone, she reached up a hand to her forehead. "Never mind. I'm just going to crash right here." She sagged in a slow sliding heap to the floor.

"Are you hurt?"

"No," she said, looking at her arms. "At least I don't

think so. I have blood on my arms, but I think it's all the dog's blood."

"Can you check?" the dispatcher said. "I'll send an ambulance if you need one."

She struggled to her feet again and walked over to the sink. She grabbed some paper towels, soaked them and proceeded to wash her arms. "I'm sore. I think the gunman hit me a couple times, trying to stop me from stabbing him." She gave a half laugh. "But I did slice him pretty good."

"What with?"

"A scalpel," she said. "I'm a vet. It's what I had handy. I cut him on his hands and on this shoulder, I think."

"I still want you to stay on the line," the woman said on the other end of the phone.

"Yeah, I'm here," Holly said, exhaustion in her voice. "And, no, I'm not hurt. I've just washed off all the blood. It's either the dog's or the gunman's."

"At least you fought him off," the dispatcher said. "Hopefully, with his wounds, he'll seek medical attention, and we can grab him then."

"He should be identifiable this way," Holly said, wiping her forehead. "But Zane … He took off after him. I don't know if he's hurt." Feeling marginally better, she walked out to the hallway, stepping over the rifle. "There is a blood trail at my door."

"Don't step in it," the dispatcher warned. "Just find a corner and stay there please."

"I'm in the back with the animals," she said. "Poor Chico is a little Chihuahua here that's been through the worst night of his life from the looks of him." She opened up the cage and reached in. Chico nuzzled her hand, looking for reassurance that it was all okay. "If you'd let me off the phone," Holly complained good-naturedly, "I could pick him up and cuddle him."

"No, you stay on the line," the dispatcher said. "The officers will be there in about four minutes."

"I hope so," she said. "I'm so tired. I'm likely to just drop from exhaustion."

"Stay awake. Stay with me," the dispatcher said, her voice sharper. "Are you sure you're not hurt?"

"I think I'm just exhausted, and the adrenaline has worn off from the shock," she said. "I'll be fine." She spent a few minutes longer, telling Chico it would be okay, stroking his head and his back until he calmed down. Then she closed his cage and walked over to check on Katch. He looked to be okay, sound asleep in the back. She wandered around the room. "Is it time yet?"

"You should hear the sirens any moment."

"I can't hear anything," Holly cried out. "Why is it taking so long?"

"Because we had to get manpower from the next station over," the dispatcher said. "Nothing in life is simple."

But then Holly heard it. "I think I hear sirens," Holly cried out, peering through the window. It wasn't morning, but there was definitely a light coming from above. "The sky is looking like morning is around the corner."

"The sun will rise in another hour," the dispatcher said. "The worst of the night is over."

"Says you," Holly said. "For all I know, this guy's waiting to pick off these cops too."

"They've been warned," the dispatcher said. "Let them do their jobs."

"I hear you," she said. "But ..."

And just then the four cop cars came streaming into the

place and parked alongside the other cop cars. She walked out to the front of the clinic and opened the front door.

"I'm hanging up now," she said to the dispatcher. "I need to talk to the cops." And she then pocketed her phone, stepping outside.

The uniformed men surrounded her. She gave them as many details as she could. She said she hadn't seen any of the cops who had shown up here in the last two hours. One of the men stepped inside with her, two others followed him. They did a quick survey of the interior of the building. One removed the rifle, and the others noticed the bloodstains leading out the door. They walked back outside.

There was a quick huddle, and, next thing she knew, they all took off. She sagged in the receptionist's chair. "And here I sit, all alone once again."

She hated to sound like *poor me*, but what she really wanted was to get Zane back and to get the hell away from this. This asshole had come back around once tonight already; she didn't want him coming back around a second time.

When her phone rang, she pulled it out of her pocket and checked it. "Zane, where are you?" she asked.

"I'm coming toward you," he said. "I see you have a lot of cops around."

"Yes, I called them. I was really worried about the other cops."

"With good reason," he said. "I found three of them. They've all been knocked unconscious."

"Make sure these new ones don't shoot you as you come toward them."

"No. I've already met up with two," he said. "We're walking in together."

"Front or back?" she asked sharply.

"Front. Apparently there's a blood trail they want to follow."

"I can't close down the vet clinic for the day," she said, "so hopefully that'll be done fast."

"You need to prepare yourself," he said, his voice gentle. "It won't be fast. None of this stuff is fast."

She hung up the phone and waited close to the front door but still in hiding. Just because he said he was coming in with two cops, she didn't know for sure who else might be coming in.

As they walked closer, she could see the outlines of three men coming toward her. "Now what do I do?" she asked out loud. She didn't recognize either of the cops, but then she hadn't seen the group who had come and dispersed right away.

"Holly," Zane called out.

She waved through the window and opened the door. "Is it safe, at least for the moment?"

He gave her a big hug. "Yes, it looks like it."

The two cops stepped into the clinic with her. One said, "We've got several ambulances coming to pick up the injured men. Four are down, but it doesn't look like anybody's dead."

"So this guy hurts five cops, and now we've got what, eight more here?" she said. "So he's gone? You know he's going to be gone. Why would he stick around?"

"We have K9 units. We're trying to get a handler to come and track him," the officer said. "He left a blood trail."

"I stabbed his hand and his shoulder with my scalpel." She looked to Zane. "You should just take Katch. Besides, this guy is likely to shoot any dog that comes after him."

Zane frowned. "But he's injured."

"Yes, he is," Holly said. "And that asshole hurt him again," she added. "I've given him a pain shot, and he's sleeping. But he's probably a good bet for tracking McAfee."

"Depends on Katch's training," Zane said. "I'm not sure tracking was part of it."

"That's the dog this guy's trying to kill?"

Holly nodded. "Yes. And he's here. I'm sure now that he's hearing strange voices he's probably awake again."

"The K9 units might take time," the guy said. "If your dog could help at all, it would be good. We need to catch this guy fast. He's obviously dangerous."

"And the asshole disarmed my security system too."

One of cops nodded. "I'll see what I can do."

"Let me check on Katch," Holly said, racing back to the holding room.

ZANE FOLLOWED HER. He was exhausted and frustrated. But, as soon as he realized the cops had been knocked out, and this McAfee guy was running free and clear again, Zane figured the asshole had taken off to take care of his own wounds. Zane himself had placed a 9-1-1 call and was told several cops were on the scene. He'd warned them not to shoot because he was out there helping the unconscious policemen. He rendezvoused up with two of the new arrivals. And now they had the other men collecting their unconscious comrades. They needed the ambulance here as soon as they could.

He wondered just how good a tracker Katch was. Zane turned around at the sound of a cop calling out to him.

He asked, "Are you capable of taking him out?"

Zane shrugged. "I'm not part of a K9 unit or anything, but I'm good with animals."

"You know we need to get a head start on this, right?"

"I know the first hour is priceless," he said. "The first hour is so important. Depends on the dog's health though. He's been beaten, abused, shot three times, broke open some of his eighty stitches tonight. So basically to hell and back because of this guy."

"Well, it might be a good thing for him then. It would give him added incentive to go after the guy."

"That's how he got hurt not even an hour ago," Holly said, walking forward slowly with a leash in her hand, leading the dog. "Katch went after him when the intruder came in hunting Katch. But, like I told you earlier, I've given him pain meds. He is, however, mobile." She walked around, Katch moving slowly but capably following her. "As you can see, he's stiff and sore, but he looks eager enough."

"He almost looks too eager," the cop said, pushing his hat off his forehead. He looked over at Zane. "Your call."

Zane nodded. "We can only try. No guarantees." He crouched in front of Katch and whispered to him, "How are you doing, boy? Are you up for this?"

Katch looked at him and seemed to gain strength. Zane leaned into the dog for a moment, then straightened and accepted the leash from Holly. "He'll be really tired when I get him back."

"I'm more concerned about the McAfee guy seeing Katch first," she admitted. "Don't let him kill Katch."

"I'll do everything I can to not let that happen," he said. He turned to look at the cops. "Need a couple men to go with me."

They both nodded. "We'll do it." They walked out the back.

Zane spoke to Katch, saying, "Come on, boy. Let's go see where the bad guy is." He led him to the blood trail, but his nose was already down and following it. Zane gave Katch the lead, urged him to go a little faster.

As he studied the dog, Zane wasn't sure how much Katch's stiff gait was from his injuries or was just from unused muscles and soreness from this most recent attack. But Katch picked up the pace eagerly. Before Zane realized it, he was jogging at Katch's side.

Zane could still see the blood himself in spots, and he was a decent tracker too. But his nose had nothing on Katch's.

The two cops stayed slightly behind him. They were better dressed than the others were for something like this, with both of them in good sneakers. Zane himself had his boots on. But he'd already pounded a ton of miles in these boots, and his navy training had kept him on drills for many, many hours. He'd be surprised if there was anything this dog could take Zane through that Katch couldn't handle. Particularly considering the dog was as injured as he was. But Katch wasn't letting his injuries slow him down. Eagerly he stepped up, pulling on his leash, faster and faster as they went from one bush to another bush, around another, across the valley, and kept right on going. And Katch wasn't slowing.

Zane glanced back to see the cops running too. He checked his time, realizing they'd probably gone two miles already. But the dog's nose was down, and Katch showed no signs of fatigue. Zane could feel his body limber and loosen as he settled into the jog. The ground was rough and uneven, but it wasn't bothering Katch. In fact, his stride seemed to relax as he followed the scent and keep striding forward as fast as he could.

No fresh blood welled from the dog's shoulder, and Zane would take that as another good sign. Maybe his injuries caused from earlier in the wee hours of this morning were more minor than Zane had thought. At least he could hope so.

When he turned to look at the cops behind him, one was languishing, and he looked pissed at himself for having to slow down. All of a sudden, the dog stopped and barked. Zane came to a stop, pulled the dog over slightly behind a tree so they could safely search the surroundings. He glanced back, making sure the cops had done the same, but there was no sign of them.

Slowly Zane gazed across the trees up ahead, finding some kind of a hut. He didn't want to call it a house or a cabin because it was more like a lean-to. If it had been hunting season, he'd have called it a hunting blind.

He crouched down low and scratched Katch's chest. "Good boy," he said. "Good boy." He didn't know if anybody was at the hut. The dog was desperate to go forward, but he heeded Zane's orders to stay.

Zane waited for a long moment, studying the structure, but he heard and saw nothing. He glanced back at the cops to see one shifting around, positioned to come up on the right side. The other went to the left side. Still, Zane had no way to know if the blind itself was just a trap.

He got up and stepped out boldly with the dog at his side. They walked forward, the dog eager, pulling on his leash, even as he listened to Zane's command to heel. Katch still had the scent, but that didn't mean McAfee was up ahead.

When Zane got to the lean-to, he stepped around to the open side. It was empty. Katch wasn't interested in the dwelling, he was looking at something else in the distance.

From the lean-to Zane saw what appeared to be someone up ahead in a tall tree, clinging to one of the lower limbs. He studied it, silently pointed it out to one of the cops and then slowly approached. Again Katch pulled at his leash. When they got twenty feet from the man, Katch started to bark. Zane saw the man lying, possibly collapsed, on the lower limb of the tree. One of the cops joined him at the base.

Zane handed off the leash and reached up. He couldn't quite make it to the branch. He looked around and shrugged. Then he backed up, took a running jump, using the tree as leverage to get up to a branch on a different side. Once there, he pulled himself up and leaned over to see what he was looking at.

"It's McAfee all right," he said. "He's out cold." He was also dripping a steady amount of blood. Zane frowned and looked at him. "He needs medical attention."

"He's dangerous as hell too," one of the cops said. "Don't approach him."

"I'm already here," Zane said, but he settled back and watched.

He was more concerned about the poor dog because, if this guy was just playing dead, his goal was to take the dog out—possibly jumping down to the ground and snapping the dog's neck, which, although not easy, could be done. And if he had a knife on him, that was another whole avenue to consider.

Zane hopped back to the ground, landing hard. He

twisted and looked up, but the unconscious man hadn't made a sound. Zane accepted the leash back and walked Katch a little farther away. But he didn't want to go. He wanted to stay. His teeth bared as he stared up at McAfee.

"That's him," Zane said. "I know you found him. Good boy."

The policemen had already called it in, but it would be difficult to find their location. Zane gave them the GPS location so the SAR team could track it and find the best way to get in.

"I'd feel better if he was secured and on the ground," Zane said.

"Me too," the closest cop said. "But we can't lift him up and get him down from there. He either has to fall from the tree, or search and rescue will have to climb up, tie him up and bring him down."

Zane studied the scene for a long moment. "It's not a bad location for him to have gotten to on his own. When you think about it, he picked a pretty decent spot."

"Yes," the second cop said. "But makes it hell on us."

Just then the man above groaned. He shifted restlessly.

"Hey," one of the cops called out. "Do you need medical attention?"

The man just groaned again. But, as he shifted, more blood oozed and ran down his arm.

Zane realized the gunman was more hurt than suspected. "Looks like one of those scalpel slices might have done a damn good job on him."

The man opened his eyes and looked around, but there was a glazed look to them. He shifted and lost his balance. He came down hard with a *thump*, then didn't move.

The two cops went to his side. One checked for weapons, and the other checked his condition.

Zane stood to the side with Katch on his leash. The dog relaxed with him, as if having McAfee in the tree had bothered him, but now, with McAfee accessible on the ground, he was less of a danger. "You just wanted to bite him yourself, didn't you?" he asked Katch gently.

The dog didn't respond with a sound or a movement, just stared, never taking his gaze off the man.

Zane walked around and said, "What the hell was his problem anyway?"

"No idea," the cop said. "But, at this rate, he'll bleed to death."

"Dammit," Zane said. "I'd like answers. Although a part of me would be totally okay with that."

The cops nodded. "Considering he's gone after cops as well, we understand that. But it's not what we're here for."

Zane checked his pockets. "I don't have any medical supplies on me." He glanced at them. "We could haul him down to the vet clinic again, but we'll be at least thirty minutes getting him back there. In the meantime, I suggest cutting up his shirt and making bandages out of that." He dipped his hand into his pocket and pulled out his pocket-knife, opened it up and handed it over.

The cops quickly cut the man's shirt into strips and used one as packing and another one to tie on his arm where Holly had managed to slice what appeared to be a slight nick to an artery. It wasn't arterial bleeding, but it was pouring out badly enough. With that one tied off, they worked on his throat, where she'd also cut him.

One officer looked back around. "We just got a dispatch saying it'll be at least forty-five minutes."

"I'm not sure he'll make it," Zane said.

"Neither are we," one of the officers said. "What's the chance of contacting the other officers down at the vet clinic?" They discussed it between each other. "Meeting them halfway? We can't get a helicopter in these dense woods. Maybe at the road?"

"It's possible." They looked at Zane and sighed. "He's got to be 250 pounds. Between us, we won't get very far."

"If you take the dog," Zane said, "I can probably carry him half the distance. But somebody has to meet us as soon as we get to the road." He stopped, turned around and looked. "Considering where we are"—he pulled out his phone, brought up the GPS on his map—"it's probably faster if we hit the road on this side. It'll be rough traveling, but it's a shorter distance, and they can meet us at that road instead."

"True." They muddled over the map for a while and then said, "Come on. Let's go. No point sitting here. He's just bleeding out faster."

On that note, Zane reached down, grabbed McAfee's arm, and, with their help, positioned him over his shoulder. He rose slowly. "Watch out for Katch," he said to the man now holding his leash. "He won't like this guy being on my shoulder."

And, sure enough, Katch was already growling.

"I'll go first," one cop said. "I'll see if I can break trail and find the easiest way forward."

Zane followed with the other cop bringing up the rear.

CHAPTER 12

"**W**HY HASN'T HE called?" she asked.

A cop sat beside her now. He'd been sent back to keep an eye on the clinic, in case the gunman escaped and circled around again.

"Because he's busy," the cop said firmly.

She groaned. She had Chico cuddled up in her lap, and the dog appeared to be, for the first time all night, content. His eyes were closed, and he lay with his head on her breast. "This poor little guy's had a terrible night," she muttered, gently stroking him.

"He looks happy now," the cop said.

She nodded and smiled. "Isn't that the truth?"

"So ... this Zane guy. How does he fit into all this?"

She explained about him coming to check on the welfare of the War Dog and finding out it had been abused and beaten and now was being hunted down.

"And he never did find out why this guy hates the dog?"

"No," she said. "We could only figure that the dog had failed to save someone close to him."

"What do you mean?"

She sighed. "I'm sorry. I'm tired, so I'm not explaining it very well."

She tried again, and this time he nodded. "The trouble is, it happens too often like that. We have therapy dogs and sniffer dogs and working dogs and search-and-rescue dogs, but they can't be held responsible for something because they didn't get the job done or other circumstances may have interrupted them. The fact that the dog has PTSD is also sad, but it's what happens to our men too. My brother's like that."

She nodded, then said, "I don't know how bad Zane's PTSD issues are or what his other health concerns are, but he is certainly struggling with being a civilian now."

"What will he do?"

"I have no clue. He's been working for Titanium Corp, but I don't know that there's any work for him here. I was hoping to keep him in town," she said with a wry smile. "We went out years ago, and then, after my husband died, I was hoping maybe to find him again."

"Maybe he'll find something here to do," he said.

"I hope so," she said sadly. "I've spent my life watching him leave."

"Did you ever consider how hard it might have been for him to get up and leave you too?" the cop asked her.

She looked at him. "No. I don't think I ever did," she said slowly. "When I was younger, all I was concerned about was the fact that he might never come home."

"That's also a concern for him."

"Then why leave?" she cried out. "Why put us through that?"

"Because he felt he needed to," he said. "And, if we didn't have men to serve, where would we be?"

"There are other men," she said, a tone of mutiny and fear in her voice, and then she sighed. "I'm still acting like that teenager. He didn't argue when I went to vet school and was gone for months at a time, but, in my head, I would be done at one point. Whereas he would never be done."

"And yet, now he is?"

"Sure," she said, "but only because he was medically discharged. His heart is still in the navy."

"I don't know about that," he said, "because he probably could have found another job within the navy. A desk job maybe. He was medically discharged, but he seems to be in good health now."

She thought about that and wondered. "Maybe, but I know it's taken him a long time to get back on his feet."

"But," the cop said, "it's all about what to do *now* and what he wants to do *now*."

She smiled and nodded. "True." She sat here for a long moment, thinking about the policeman's words. "I never really thought about how hard it was for Zane because I figured, if it was hard, he wouldn't have done it."

"How hard was it going to vet school?" he asked. "Leaving your family and friends, leaving for months at a time? And how hard was the actual work?"

"It was terrible," she admitted. "Like seriously ugly. It took me probably into the second or third year before I adjusted to it."

"But you still did it, didn't you?"

"Of course, because that's what I needed to do to live my dream life," she said. Then there was silence when she sagged in the chair. "Okay, that wasn't very nice."

"Maybe, but hopefully it helped you see things from his point of view."

With that, some of her bitterness toward Zane disappeared. "Okay, now I don't feel very good about myself. I'm really not a mean person."

"And then there's the other thing. Didn't you say you

married his brother?"

"Yes," she said wearily.

"That might make it very hard for Zane," the cop said. "I don't know how I'd feel if my brother married my girlfriend, except to figure I was done and wasn't going back. To a lot of brothers, that would be like the biggest betrayal. In my case, I know I couldn't handle it," he admitted. "It would be something too intimate and almost twisted having a girlfriend that my own brother already slept with."

"That doesn't sound like what I want to hear either," she said.

"Maybe not," he said, "but, if you don't talk to Zane about it, you won't ever understand what he's struggling with."

"Maybe." Now she felt really bad about it all.

"And then maybe he's fine with it," the cop said. "Second chances and all that."

"Well, I hope so," she said, "because I don't think I can handle him leaving again."

"Then he needs to know that," the cop said, standing up. "He needs to know you're not going to take that anymore. And you have to consider, what if he says he has to? What will you do about it?"

She winced. "You're talking about me leaving here, aren't you?"

"If he can't stay, are you ready to leave with him? Because you say you can't stand for him to leave again, so your choices are to watch him leave, get him to stay or you going with him. Which is it going to be?" He turned and walked away.

She stared at him, almost hating him for voicing the words. She had already considered whether she could leave, but she wasn't giving Zane a choice in the matter either. And that was probably wrong. Not *probably*, it was *definitely* wrong. And once again it didn't make her feel very good. Had she always been so selfish? She didn't want it to be that way. She wanted to be somebody who could see his side. But she hadn't been that person lately. She'd been wrapped up in her own pain and grief, maybe looking at him as a solution. And yet, he wasn't a solution. He was what she'd always wanted. Somehow she had to make that work again.

Just then the other cop stepped back inside. "Just so you know, they're on the way out of the woods, carrying your attacker. He's unconscious and bleeding."

She stared at him. "That's good, I guess."

He nodded. "You nicked some decent blood vessels when you attacked him."

"While he was attacking me, trying to shoot Zane and the dog and me?" she said defensively, with heat behind her words.

He held up his hands. "Don't worry. Nobody's blaming you. They're heading to the nearest road so they can get picked up by the ambulance, which hopefully will be in the next ten to fifteen minutes."

"So it's over?" She wanted to believe it, but ...

"I hope so," he said. "They've got the guy anyway. We're collecting the rest of the officers, and I'm sure there'll be a hell of a lot of paperwork over something like this. But it looks like, for the clinic and for the dog, it's over."

"Can I open the clinic tomorrow?"

"You mean, today?"

"Yes," she said. "It's a full business day."

He frowned. "Let me talk to the others about it."

He came back ten minutes later and said, "We've got a

team coming in. They'll photograph, take fingerprints and blood samples. They'll do their best, but they need at least three or four hours."

She looked down at her watch. "It would be best if they could be done and gone by nine o'clock."

"We'll see," he said. "It's not my decision." And then he was gone again.

She sagged into a chair, wondering when she would see Zane again. She couldn't believe they'd found the shooter. Good for Katch, that he'd managed to track McAfee. But then Katch had more motivation than most other animals and the most incentives.

With that news, she could feel the fatigue hitting her. To know Zane and Katch were only about fifteen minutes away from the road, she should see Zane in hopefully another half hour.

She thought about it, then realized maybe she should lie down and grab a power nap so she could handle what was coming. There would likely be a ton of questions and a ton of people in her space.

She walked back into the treatment room and returned Chico to his cage. He went willingly, curling up in the back, prepared to have a good nap. Then she walked into her office and stretched out on the cot. Definitely not time for a full-blown sleep session.

She lay down, closed her eyes and was out instantly.

THE COPS PULLED the cruiser into the clinic parking lot and let Zane out. The front door was unlocked, and the place was full of people. He stopped and stared. "What's going on?"

"We're trying to get through the forensics," one of the men said, "so she can open the clinic today."

He smiled at that. "Thank you for even considering it."

"Hey, we're doing the best we can. She helped save our men. We're trying to help save her business."

Zane stepped inside, watching as the men moved through the place. "I guess it's still a few hours until she opens up for the day."

"Yes. She asked for a deadline of nine a.m., if we could."

"Where is she?"

"In her office, sleeping," one of the men said. "I've already fingerprinted in there. She never once moved."

He nodded and stepped through the room. "You guys okay if I bring in the dog?"

"The dog looks exhausted, but absolutely," one guy said.

Moving the very tired Katch with him back to the office, Zach stepped inside and closed the door. Katch walked over to the cot and sniffed Holly. She murmured and rolled over.

"Katch, lie down," Zane whispered.

Katch just looked at him. But he slowly sagged to the floor beside Holly. She never woke up. Zane walked to her chair and wondered about sitting and sleeping there. He decided lying down beside Katch was probably the better answer.

He sat down beside the dog. His tail wagged, and, as Zane lay here, the dog reached up his paw and dropped it gently on his shoulder. "Right, boy," he said. He closed his eyes. He'd spent enough years training himself to sleep when he could because, on a lot of navy missions, there was just no getting eight hours for anybody.

He lay here half asleep until he heard her start to wake.

"Zane, is that you?" she murmured.

"It is," he said.

"Are you hurt? Are you okay?" She bolted upright and stared down at him.

He opened his eyes and smiled up at her. "We're both okay. Katch did a great job," he said, reaching out to gently stroke Katch's forehead and nose. "He's pretty tired, and that'll probably slow his healing, but he did a fantastic job."

Holly leaned over and gently cuddled the dog. "I'm so happy for you, Katch. Talk about redeeming qualities."

"I think the other guys were pretty impressed too," he said. "But I have to admit, I'm done. Are you capable of actually working today?"

"It's just office visits, thankfully no surgeries, but I'm certainly tired," she said. "It's a half day, being Saturday, so that's a good thing."

"So you're working from nine till noon?"

"Nine to one," she said.

"And then we'll crash, right?"

"Not at all," she said. "You'll crash now. I'll come home when I'm done after the morning visits."

"No," he said, "absolutely not. You've got maybe two hours left before it's time to open. You and I'll crash here. At nine o'clock you'll get up, be the good vet, and, at one o'clock, we'll go home." He closed his eyes, crossing his arms over his chest.

"You look like you're posed to be buried," she said with a chuckle.

"Nope, not quite," he said.

"How badly did I hurt him?" she asked.

He heard the worry in her voice. "I don't think you killed him, and that's too damn bad. Because somebody like that won't stop."

"But they'll put him in jail now, won't they?"

"He's getting medical treatment first," he said. "And then jail, yes. But it's hard to know that guy's always out there. Always waiting."

"But, if he's jailed long enough," she said, "then he could be in jail longer than the dog is likely to live."

He thought about that for a long moment, then nodded. "A sad thought but true enough. Maybe that's all we need to focus on then."

"I'd say so," she said. She lay back down again. "I am so tired."

"Exactly. Close your eyes and sleep."

"Only if you do," she said with a laugh.

"If we wake up early enough," he said, "I suggest we get a big breakfast. In the meantime, it's all about sleep." And he closed his eyes and crashed.

CHAPTER 13

S HE WALKED TO the door with Mrs. Mohnishe and smiled at the huge ginger-colored tomcat. Well, he was no longer a tomcat but still all cat as he walked out the door on a leash with his owner. "You have a great weekend," Holly called out.

Mrs. Mohnishe waved at her. "You too."

Holly headed back into the reception area to see Mittle sitting there with the stack of files she was organizing in order to close up the clinic. "Everyone is gone. Can we leave?"

"Yep. Everybody's done and gone," Mittle said. "Including all the cops and all the forensic people. Everybody but one."

Holly didn't have to ask who was the one. She knew Zane was still crashed in her office. She walked back into the office to see him just waking up.

He smiled and said, "Is it time to go home?"

"It sure as hell is," she said, stifling a yawn. "I'm just not so sure what to do about Katch."

"Let's take him home and see how he does in your yard."

She frowned. "I'm not keeping him."

"Maybe not," he said, "but I am."

She stared at him, a light growing inside her. "What does that mean?"

"Not sure yet. But when a bond is formed, you don't dismiss it that easily," he said with a smile. "Now let's get some food, just pick it up I guess, because we have the dog with us, and go home."

He stood and looked down at Katch, still sleeping on the floor. Then he rolled over; his head was up, his ears up too. Zane asked, "Do you want to go home, boy?"

He gave a short bark and hopped to his feet.

"I should check him over first," Holly said.

"I suggest you bring whatever he needs home," Zane said. "Medication for pain, for the rest of today and over-night, so we can give it to him there."

She nodded. "Give me a few minutes, and I'll collect some stuff." She turned around and headed into the back room, where she grabbed some pain medication for the dog and another dose of antibiotics.

She came back, and, with Zane holding Katch—even though he didn't fight them—Holly gave him a shot of the antibiotics and another of pain meds.

"I'll bring more pain medication home with us," she said, "and another dose of the antibiotics. We should be good to go for the rest of today."

"Make sure we're good to go until Monday," Zane said. "As much as I don't have a problem with you having the clinic, I really don't want to come back today or tomorrow if we don't have to."

She smiled up at him. "I can't think of anything better." She went back, packed up a small bag and grabbed her purse, then headed out. "Come on. Mittle's leaving too."

They walked out to the front, set the security alarm, which the one policeman got working again, locked the door, and stepped outside.

She took several deep breaths, looked up at the sky and said, "I really want to just go home and crash."

"Do we have enough food?"

"There's got to be," she said. "We'll make do. I grabbed some dog food from the clinic too. We should be good."

He motioned to the back of the pickup. "Don't really want him to travel in the bed of the truck."

"You've got room in the back seat," she said.

And that was what they did, helping Katch get in the back seat of the double-cab pickup. Zane turned on the engine, waited until Holly had her seat belt buckled up and then headed home.

"*Home,*" she said with a whisper. "I don't think it's ever sounded quite so good."

"I hear you," he said. "I really want to hear from the cops that it's all done, that this guy is secured."

She looked at him. "He has to be secured?"

"No, he doesn't," he said drily, "But all kinds of shit can happen. I'll contact the cops when we get back to your place."

They would be home within a few minutes, and she couldn't wait. As she opened the truck door and hopped out, Katch barked from the back seat. She opened the back door for him and helped him get down. With a leash attached to the simple collar, she led him up to the front door and stopped, looking behind her.

Zane was searching the area. She was surrounded by trees on all sides, even the driveway that wove its path through the trees. She called out, "What are you looking for?"

He gave her a shuttered look. "Anything and nothing."

On that note she turned and walked into her house. She

didn't want to think about that asshole coming after her and the dog. The cops had him. He was injured. That should be the end of it.

Inside, she put her stuff on the counter and walked over to put on the teakettle. Zane might want coffee, but she was desperate for a good cup of tea.

She stared out the back and then turned to watch as Katch wandered around the inside of her house, sniffing everything. He was still bloody, but that would be a little hard to clean up for now. He was also quite tired.

He's looking for a place to lie down. Holly walked to the front closet and pulled out a blanket she kept for cold evenings when she wanted to just sit outside. She folded it into a thick pad and laid it on the living room floor. Katch collapsed on top of it.

She squatted in front of him, gently scratching him on the head. "You just rest, boy. You just rest."

She heard Zane coming in the front door, his heavy footsteps welcoming as he walked in.

He came through to the kitchen, looking for her, and saw her beside Katch. He smiled. "How is he doing?"

"Exhausted, needing to heal. He requires rest and time to recover," she said. "At least a week."

He nodded. "I'm not at all surprised. He took the brunt of this last attack. But he also gave as good as he got." He stopped, turned and looked at her again and smiled. "And then so did you."

She just shrugged. "Honestly, I grabbed the closest weapon I could find, and I just started slashing."

"You slashed pretty good." He looked at the teakettle. "Did you just put that on?"

"I did, why?"

"Would you mind if I put on coffee?"

"Go for it," she said. "Make yourself at home."

She watched from Katch's side as Zane bustled about the kitchen and efficiently put on a small pot of coffee. At least he didn't have a problem with making what he wanted.

When he was done, he crouched and eyed the wounds on Katch's body. "He's been through a lot, hasn't he?"

"Too much," Holly announced. She hopped to her feet. "And so have I. I need food too." She opened the fridge.

Zane stood behind her. "There's at least enough for sandwiches, if you have bread."

She nodded. "That might be all there is."

He bent and pulled out the small freezer drawer in the bottom and found steaks and chops and some chicken breasts. But also a couple packages of ham were up a level in the bottom drawer in the fridge. He brought them out. "How about a ham and egg sandwich?"

She smiled. "That sounds wonderful."

Together they made a simple lunch, and, within a few minutes, they were both sitting down to eat—her with one sandwich and him with two.

As soon as she was done, she yawned. "You know what? I slept a lot, but all that chaos ..."

"It's adrenaline," he said. "Nap time."

She glanced at her watch. "It's two o'clock. I'm scared to sleep too much, then not sleep tonight."

"Then set an alarm," he said. "That's not a hardship, is it?"

"No, but it's not the same as waking up on your own," she said with a smile. "I swear alarm clocks are the demon's tools."

He chuckled at that. "I'll clean up our lunch," he said.

"You go on up."

"Okay," she said, almost stumbling on her way. She stopped in the hallway and turned to look back at him. "And then we'll talk."

He raised an eyebrow. "About what?"

His tone was so neutral that she knew he already understood just what the subject would be. "You already know," she said, "so make sure you're available for that conversation—which needs to happen regardless."

"Does it?" he asked.

"Absolutely," she said. "You're not getting out of it this time."

He smiled, and she headed up to her room.

Upstairs she took off her outer layer of clothing and, just in her underwear, crawled under the covers. She didn't know how long she'd sleep, but she was willing to give it a go. She curled up in a ball, closed her eyes, thought about Zane downstairs cleaning up the kitchen, and she smiled. "At least he knows where he belongs," she said with a chuckle.

And let sleep pull her under.

ZANE WASN'T VERY good with those kinds of conversations. As a matter of fact, they always seemed to take him a direction he didn't want to go. But, as he stood moodily out in the backyard, he knew it needed to happen, and sooner was better than later.

His phone buzzed, a call from his brother. He answered it. "Hey, Butch, what's up?"

"You apparently," his brother said. "What's all this I hear about poor Holly's clinic getting broken into, not once but twice?"

"Somebody was after the dog I came here to check on," Zane said and explained everything.

His brother's response was, "I don't give a damn about the dog. What's happening to Holly?"

"Not a whole lot now," he said. "She's taking a nap. The guy broke into her clinic to get at the dog."

"Reggie should have kept the dog."

"We were trying to get the dog away from the guy who's been hunting him," Zane said patiently.

"You should let him have it. The dog is too much trouble. Chances are he'll be put down anyway."

"Why is that?" Zane asked, his temper sparking. He'd fought long and hard to save this dog. The last thing he wanted to do was listen to anymore attitude from people like his brother.

"Because he's obviously dangerous," he said. "For God's sake, it's just a dog." He hung up.

Zane put away his phone, hating that, once again, something so simple as saving a dog, a veteran, would drive a wedge between him and his family. It didn't seem to matter what the issue, Zane was always on the wrong side. When it came to serving his country, the others not only had argued against it, they'd mocked him for it, not understanding why he wanted to do it. Now here he was with just a simple case of saving a dog from cruel mistreatment. But, once again, his dad and brother were on the other side. Zane assumed his father wouldn't change his mind from the words he'd spoken just a couple days ago.

Zane was pretty sure, at this point, his brother called to let Zane know how Butch felt about putting Holly in danger. That wasn't what Zane or Holly needed right now, but Zane wouldn't be surprised to have his father call and give him shit too.

Zane brought Katch back inside. He sipped his coffee, realizing Holly hadn't bothered to make her cup of tea. Whereas he himself had a small pot of coffee to drink on his own. Katch's tail wagged ever-so-slightly as Zane walked toward him and sat down on the living room couch beside Katch. "It's all right, boy. We're doing okay. You just need to get your strength back."

The best thing for Zane and Katch would be to find a place to live a long way away from here. Thankfully all the policemen involved in the takedown of McAfee had already mentioned how they were petitioning to have the citizen complaints against Katch overruled by their own commendations. Zane felt good about that but wondered whether the rest of the guys in blue would accept him and Katch without proof of their worth, whether seen as veterans or not.

People around the area had very long memories, and Zane didn't know how the other locals felt about him protecting Katch, but Zane knew his father and brother wouldn't go easy on him. But why? They didn't have anything to do with Zane anyway.

Even if he did stay, he couldn't imagine he'd have much of a relationship with either of them. If they did see each other, Zane would have to tell them that the subject of killing dogs was taboo, especially when it came to Katch individually. They would have to agree to disagree or just not see each other again. That wasn't much of a threat except for where it involved Holly. Zane would tell his dad and his brother to honor Holly's profession and to leave this subject unmentioned.

After all, when Zane was gone for his years in the navy,

even the last year as he recuperated, Dad and Butch hadn't bothered to call or write, so Zane doubted they would do the cozy backyard barbecues on weekends just because he was nearby either.

In a way, it saddened him. Brody was the only one their father was close to, and even they weren't very close. Not in a healthy or normal way. Three boys and one drunken father. Each of the boys trying to grow up, to understand the world around them, without killing themselves or their father in the process. So much anger was involved in that kind of a childhood environment, but Zane had lost most of his in the navy. Nothing like doing sit-ups and ten-mile runs to exhaust his anger—or at least otherwise occupy his time when he was awake.

He wasn't sure about the next step, the forgiveness part. But he admitted he was working on it.

Zane hadn't even understood he had anything to forgive until he saw his father again, and then Zane realized all he could do at this point was accept that his father was an old man who wanted nothing but to sit in his own pile of negativity. Zane didn't have to join his father in that useless and unproductive endeavor. Unfortunately, it looked like his eldest brother was going the same route. Zane had hoped Sandra would be a soothing effect for Butch. Zane just didn't know about that now. It might not be enough.

And what about him? Here he was in Holly's house, looking at the world from a very different place than he had before. He knew she wanted to resume their relationship, and he hated to admit her having married his brother was a stumbling block for him. And it was his own stumbling block. He couldn't blame her for moving on. He couldn't blame his brother for wanting her. She was beautiful, smart, and funny. The fact that they had actually made it, gotten married, and been happy for a couple years was a kindness, in his mind, to both of them. He didn't want his brother to have gone to his grave unhappy, and, in the years that Zane was gone, he didn't want Holly to be unhappy either. If Zane and Holly had been together, and he'd died, he'd want her to move on too.

Essentially it was the same thing. They'd broken up, and she'd moved on. The fact that it was with his brother hurt, and yet, Zane could also see how that the connection was already there. She was, in a way, primed for that relationship because Brody had been around them a lot when they dated, when they were a couple. Brody just quickly jumped in once Zane was gone.

Maybe that was a resentment he felt toward his brother, even though he had died and now could never make amends verbally. Zane felt in his heart that sense of his brother taking advantage of Holly, but, like she had said, they'd been happy. She'd eventually loved Brody, but she still loved Zane too.

He wasn't sure how that worked, didn't know that he really wanted to inspect it too closely either.

He could hear sounds upstairs and realized she was tossing and turning, probably not sleeping worth a damn. And that was too bad because she needed it. Of all the things she needed right now, she—and Katch—needed sleep.

He wandered out into the backyard again, leaving the door open in case Katch wanted to come out, taking a seat on the wooden bench. She had an acre here and was less than ten minutes to the center of town, and that was just enough space to know you had neighbors out there, but they weren't close enough to get in your face. The fact that she also had a ton of trees helped give her more privacy. He couldn't see the neighbors on either side. He knew they were there because he had passed their driveways. But he'd never been down those driveways to see who lived there or in what kind of residences. If he walked her property, he could probably see more, but he'd have to care to do that, and he didn't really care at the moment. He was too torn up with thoughts about what he was supposed to do now.

Speaking of which, he pulled out his phone and called Badger. When there was no answer, he left a message. "I need to bring you up to date on the last twelve hours."

Hearing a noise behind him, he shuffled his position on the bench to see Katch slowly walking toward him. He smiled, seeing the valiance in his gaze, the lightness on his features. His body was relaxed, sensing no danger, not that ever-present wariness that showed when he was hurt so badly. "Hey, Katch. I'm glad to see you out here."

Katch's tail wagged as he moved toward Zane slowly but steadily. The shepherd limped on his sore leg, which was to be expected, and he had a bit of a hitch in his back as he walked, as if he were clenching against the upcoming pain. But it wasn't long before he nudged his head into Zane's fingers.

Zane gently stroked his nose. "You've had a pretty shitty life for the last bit. We're going to make it a lot better though."

Katch didn't seem to mind whatever Zane said. Katch just closed his eyes and let Zane gently stroke, scrubbing the dog's neck and under his chin, rubbing his ears. Zane could feel some of his own strain and stress roll off his back. How long since he'd had a few days like these last two? Since he had arrived, there had been nonstop action. But it was over now.

Thinking of which, he pulled out his phone and sent a text to the cops, the one in particular who he'd worked with, asking about the condition of the policeman who got shot and of the gunman they'd picked up. Instead of a text back, the phone rang.

"Hey, yeah, our fellow buddy in blue will be fine but has to stay overnight in the hospital. As for the gunman responsible for shooting that policeman, he's doing okay. At least he'll live. He lost a lot of blood, and he's in intensive care, but we've got him under high security."

"Good to know," Zane said. "I'd hate to have that on Holly's shoulders, thinking she might have killed him."

"At the moment he's holding, and we're after him for shooting one cop and injuring the others. I know you're after him for the dog but ..."

"I know," Zane said. "If animal cruelty can be one of the charges, that would be nice, but I understand knocking out the cops and shooting one will bring much bigger charges."

"Glad you understand. I hope Holly will too. It's tough enough on all of us," he said. "The good news is, all of the cops will recover. Oh, and we did find the trigger for why he suddenly went off the cliff. His brother, a war vet had life support turned off a few weeks ago. He blamed the dog, although we can't be sure the same dog was even involved, I don't think that detail even mattered to him—just when he heard somehow that this one was part of the War Dog program he couldn't think of anything else but killing it."

"That is good news, indeed," Zane said with a smile, feeling the sun break out of the clouds above him. "Makes the rest of today a hell of a lot better than it started out."

"Right. What a change a few hours makes. Anyway, we'll

need to get your statements on the latest events. Do you want us to come later this afternoon or tomorrow?"

"Tomorrow," he said. "Holly's sleeping right now. Hopefully she'll sleep through the day. She didn't get much rest over the last couple nights."

"I know she didn't," the cop said. "I'll pop by in the morning then." He hung up.

The phone rang again—Badger calling back.

"Sorry about that," Badger said. "I was on another call. You found Katch?"

Zane chuckled. "He's got his chin resting on my knee. Holly's sleeping after the double attacks we've had. That was pretty hot and steady action, without much of a break or downtime."

"Sounds like you've got what you need right now," Badger said. "So was I right about sending you back to Maine?"

"Maybe," he compromised. "I'm not saying you won this round ... but maybe."

"Are you looking for work and wanting to stay?" Badger asked.

Zane frowned. "I didn't say I was staying," he protested not quite ready to share his thoughts with Badger.

"Neither did you say you were leaving," Badger said, "so I'm just tossing that out there. If you are interested in staying, we might find work for you."

At that Zane shook his head. "You don't have to make up jobs for me. I'm a fully capable male. I can find jobs on my own."

Badger howled. "You know better than that. We don't pussyfoot around here. It doesn't matter what limbs you might be missing or what kind of condition you might be dealing with, we don't take on pity cases. I meant that we need someone to run point from the East Coast. If you're interested, you could be like a satellite office."

In spite of himself, he was interested. "What kind of stuff?"

"No clue yet," Badger said. "But we did have a conversation with a cop from your local precinct because they were checking up on you. They mentioned something about you going into the police business or into the security business, and we were wondering if you wanted to be hired for contract work."

"Like a contract cop?" He shook his head. "That doesn't sound viable."

Badger chuckled. "No, but maybe as an investigator. They hire those on a contract basis when they get flooded with cases."

Zane straightened, his interest picking up. "Huh. I've never considered something like that. But it is kind of the work I used to do."

"I know," Badger said. "That's why I brought it up. Of course it wouldn't be just for your local precinct. You could be needed a lot of other places. Government offices all over hire independent consultants like us to give them a hand when they're overwhelmed."

"That might be something we could talk about," Zane said. "As long as it's a real job."

"Would I give you anything but a real job?" Badger asked. "The job might be fluid at the moment, but it's a real job."

"I do have some security work in my background too."

"That's right. You were in NCIS for a long time, weren't you?"

"Yeah," Zane said. "I don't talk about it much. Most often I get a negative response when I do."

"Yep," Badger said. "But it's perfect for our needs and perfect for law enforcement agencies. So why don't we check into it to see what training you might need and what the job opportunities look like from our end? If you're interested, that is."

"I'm interested," he said. "I just don't know how much work there would actually be."

"It depends on Katch too," Badger said.

"What does it have to do with him?"

"I presume you're keeping him."

Zane groaned. "Yes, but I don't have a place for him."

"Is he trainable?"

"He's very trainable," he said, affectionately stroking Katch's nose. "He is already well trained, follows commands well. He just needs a bit of a tune-up."

"Exactly," Badger said. "So you know how most law enforcement agencies are short on trained K9s too."

"You mean, like search and rescue?"

"That's just one avenue. How about a sniffer dog? Or how about a mascot dog, one that walks through the schools and lets people know the dogs are out there to help people."

"A community-service thing?" he asked. "Remember I'm not much of a people person."

"You don't know what you are anymore," Badger said. "Anyway, I'll take that as a yes. I'll get back to you in a bit." And he hung up.

"What was that?" Holly's voice called out to him.

He turned to see her standing on the patio, a cup of coffee in her hand. He got up, intending to walk toward her.

She waved at him and said, "I'm coming."

He sat back down and watched her head to him.

CHAPTER 14

S HE'D WOKEN UP after a short but intense nap and had called out to him. When she got no answer, she'd run downstairs. It had been such a relief to see him talking on the phone; the sight of Katch cuddling with Zane just about broke her heart. She hoped he wouldn't abandon Katch ... or her. She hadn't realized how much that panic was still ingrained in her.

She'd poured herself a cup of coffee, wondering who he was talking to. She stepped outside, not wanting to intrude, but wanting to join him and the dog if possible. She didn't know if the conversation was something private or not. She heard something about him not making any decisions but also that Katch was trainable.

Katch, at the moment, looked like he was in a state of nirvana. He leaned against Zane's leg, his head resting on his knee, while Zane gently stroked his face and nose and ears. This was what the dog needed, somebody to care for him, somebody to make him part of a family.

She strolled toward them, wondering how to approach the subject. "Who was that?"

"My boss," he said, his tone short.

Her heart sank. She sagged down on the bench beside him. "So, you are leaving then?" Even with her best efforts, her tone was sad, abrupt, hard.

He shook his head. "No. He was wondering if I was interested in staying."

She looked at him, hope in her eyes. "He what?"

"Yeah. Apparently the local cops called him, wanting some background on me and probably a reference to make sure I wasn't some crazy dude. So they contacted him, and, through that conversation, the cop said they were thinking about hiring some security men to help out. Obviously they weren't talking about law officers, but they could be special investigators." He waved his hand. "I don't know exactly in what capacity, but my boss said there was probably work here if I was interested. I figured it was a makeshift job because Badger and his team have done an awful lot for vets like me—but not necessarily, you know, real jobs. I think it's almost like they make up the jobs."

"Creating jobs is a business in itself," she announced. "And honestly, if there was work like that, would that be okay?"

He looked down at Katch and smiled. "One of Badger's last questions was, if I thought Katch was trainable."

"Trainable?"

"Yes. Maybe I can train him to do search-and-rescue work and much more, or even community patrol stuff, walking through the classrooms and the park, letting people get to know about dogs in law enforcement, what Katch's history is, things like that."

She looked at him in delight. "You know what? I think that's a perfect role for Katch, especially as a therapy animal. It would help people understand he has therapy issues too."

"Exactly, and the devastation on animals that comes out of accidents and the military workforce too." He shrugged. "I don't think they have any specific work in mind for me, and I don't think they have a job yet, contract or otherwise. But I think they were feeling me out to see if I would be interested in doing that."

"And would you go back and forth?"

"As a company man, I would, yes," he said. "But I'm not sure yet. Again, no answers, just something to think about."

"*Good* thoughts?" she asked slowly.

He glanced down at her, and his lips twitched. "Possibly."

Her smile widened. "And with that segue," she said, "I guess it might be time to talk about us?" She watched as he withdrew. "I'm not trying to pressure you, but what about our relationship?" Then all those words she had never shared with Zane came out in a flurry, as if she were afraid if she didn't say them now, they wouldn't come out. Even those painful words that the one cop had told her to mention, she even added them in. She leaned back and let out a heavy sigh. "Whew. That was hard to get out."

"It didn't sound like it was hard," he said. "It came out in a flood."

"Yep," she said. "Better to get it out instead of letting it stick in my throat, forever silent."

"I don't have any problems with a relationship. In fact, it would be nice to see where this goes." His voice was cautious though.

"I'd love that, but …" She reached over, picking up his huge hand in hers. "We have a lot of history, both good and bad, but we also have a future. It's up to us to make it good or bad."

"I'm all about the future." He wrapped an arm around her shoulders and tugged her close.

She leaned over, her head snuggling against his chest as

she petted Katch's forehead.

"But I don't have a job," he reminded her. "I don't have a place to live," he added. "And apparently, I come with baggage."

She started to chuckle. "If you mean Katch, I'm not sure if he's your baggage or my baggage. At the moment, it seems like he's baggage for both of us."

Katch had lifted a paw and placed it on top of Holly's knee, as if making sure Holly knew she was wanted and welcome too.

"There is that point too," he said, squeezing her shoulders gently. He dropped a kiss on her temple. "It would be like going back in time though. I'm not sure that's ever a good idea."

"We can't go back in time," she said, "because ... let's think about this. Everything in life is about moving forward. That's something we really need to do. So it's not about bringing who we were forward but about reconnecting as who we are now, then moving forward." They sat in silence for a moment, before she continued. "It's because I married your brother, isn't it?" She reared back slightly and looked up at him. "But you have to know, if I had any idea this day would come ..."

He reached up and pressed a finger against her lips, stopping her for the moment. "In the beginning," he said, "I definitely had a lot of anger and disquiet over the fact you married my kid brother." He turned to stare out at the woods around them. "But I've come to an understanding."

"Understanding what?" she asked, puzzled. "I need clarity here because this is too big an issue to ignore or to bypass. It'll always be between us if we can't clear it up now."

"I came to understand that, if you and I had been the

ones who had married, and *I* had died, exactly what is it I would have wanted for you? And I would have wanted you to move on, to find happiness, to not be alone," he said. "It took me a while to realize, even though you and I had broken up, that's exactly what I wanted for you anyway. The fact that you chose my brother was very disturbing because it was like he was stepping into my shoes, the younger brother trying to take what the older brother had. But, with his passing, that changed everything yet again. I'm sorry for him in that he died so young, but I'm grateful for you for making his last few years happy."

She could feel her heart melting at his words. It wasn't what she'd expected him to say, wasn't in any way what she'd thought he would say. But it was good. It was very good. She reached up and kissed his cheek. "Thank you. I needed to hear that." And just as she started to pull away, he changed the angle of their faces and kissed her.

When he finally lifted his head, she looked up at him, her heart melting, her body on fire and her brain completely turned to mush. She opened her mouth once, then twice, and then just gave it up, wrapping her arms tight around his chest and cuddling in close.

"You okay?" he asked.

She smiled and nodded. "I'm fine. But, to be honest, I wish we were not out in my backyard but tucked up in my bed." She felt the jolt through his body at her words and leaned back. "Surely that's where you wanted this to go too?"

"I've always wanted that," he said. "There's been nothing as complete in my life as making love to you."

Again his words seared right through her heart, lighting it on fire. She'd always loved him. But everything he said just made her love him a little more. She glanced down at Katch, who was now lying at their feet. "I think he needs new pain meds," she said worriedly. She touched the dog.

Katch just looked up at her. Instead of being in pain, he looked exhausted.

"No," she announced. "He just needs to go to bed." She tossed Zane a sideways look. "Like I think we need to do."

He was on his feet. "You won't get an argument out of me."

She chuckled and called Katch.

Katch struggled to his feet and stood, swaying.

Zane gave a strangled exclamation, swooped down and gently scooped his arms underneath the dog's chest and belly and lifted him carefully. The trio slowly walked up to the house.

"Bring him to the master bedroom, and I'll make a bed for him on the floor there. I don't really want to leave him alone."

"Lead the way," Zane said.

She shut the back door in the kitchen, locked it and headed up the stairs ahead of him. "I hope he'll be okay," she whispered.

"If you're that worried, do we need to check him out further?"

"No, I can see it's sheer exhaustion. He's done too much," she said, fretting. "He really needs several days' rest and lots of nourishment. I'll mix up some vitamins in a bit," she said, looking down at the dog. "It would be hard for him to eat anything right now."

She grabbed extra blankets out of the top shelf of her closet and laid them on the floor. Gently Zane lowered the dog, and Katch didn't even murmur. He shifted slightly to get more comfortable and then stretched out and closed his eyes. Just to reassure herself, she bent down and checked his pulse and then his chest.

"His pulse is strong. His breathing is regular. He's simply exhausted," she announced. She stood back up and stepped away.

Zane's arms came around from behind.

She leaned into them and whispered, "It feels like we have a family all of a sudden."

"I'm surprised you don't have half a dozen animals," he said. "You always loved them."

"It was part of what we had together," she said. "But, if you remember, Brody didn't like animals. They were dirty. He had a lot of the family opinion about that." She was grateful when Zane's body didn't stiffen at the mention of his brother.

"I remember that," he said in a lazy voice. "I was always the crazy animal-loving brother."

"Apparently still are," she said with a light chuckle. She turned in his arms to look up at him, sliding her hands up over his chest to gently stroke his neck. "Did I tell you how glad I am that you came back into my life?"

"No," he said, his tone picking up with interest. "I have to admit that makes me curious."

"Curious?" she asked, a tiny frown playing at the corner of her lips. "How does that work?"

"That's what I was going to ask you." He nudged her toward the bed. "I was wondering just how grateful you are."

Instantly she understood, and laughter bubbled up and out. "*Very* grateful." She stood on tiptoes to kiss his chin. "Even more grateful than I could imagine." She added kisses down his neck. Her hand slid from his chest to his waist and under his T-shirt, coming up to stroke his belly. When he sucked in his breath, she smiled and leaned back. "Still so ticklish?"

He glared at her mockingly. "No," he said.

She tickled the inside of his belly, and that got him started.

He picked her up and tossed her on the bed. "Oh, no you don't. Of course I'm still ticklish." He grinned. "Are you? As I recall, you have several ticklish spots."

She backed up off the bed, screaming in laughter. "No, no, no, no. I'm sorry. I'm sorry. I won't tickle you."

He just smiled. As he stood in front of her, he slowly pulled his T-shirt up over his head.

She stared, fascinated, wincing as she saw the scars and scrapes on his body. She kneeled on the bed, her fingers stroking the wounds from the years he'd spent away from her. "I don't even want to ask how you got these. But back to that being grateful part." She leaned forward and kissed a particularly large and rigid scar. "Grateful you're alive. Grateful you survived all these traumas. Grateful your body healed as well as it did."

He shuddered and pulled her chin up. "I'm glad for all the gratitude because, at the moment, I'm feeling pretty damn thankful myself. But you're wearing an awful lot of clothing."

She smiled. "You took off your T-shirt, so I could do the same." She crossed her arms, grabbed her T-shirt and pulled it over her head.

"That doesn't quite work," he said, "because my chest is bare."

She raised her eyes at his logic, looked down to see the lacy scraps covering her breasts and snickered. "I could take this off, or I could leave it on." She bounced to her feet so she stood on the bed. Her fingers went to the clasp of her jeans.

His hands went to his jeans. Together they slowly lowered the material, both of them kicking their pants into different corners of the room.

She smiled. "Now I'm down to two pieces." She motioned at him. "You're down to three."

He chuckled. "That's cheating. You weren't wearing socks to begin with."

"Maybe not," she said, "but I had more under my T-shirt than you did."

He took off both socks and then stood there, waggling his eyebrows at her.

She smiled, reached behind her and loosened the clasp on her bra, letting the material fall forward. She still stood on the bed, while he stood on the floor, putting her slightly taller than him.

He stepped back for a moment, his breath releasing in a slow and heavy exhale. "I'd forgotten," he whispered, his hands reaching up to cup her breasts. "I forgot just how absolutely perfect you are." He leaned forward and kissed first one breast and then the other, his hands gently stroking, caressing, lifting the weight in his palms and just loving the feel of her breasts.

When his hand stroked to the side of her ribs and down, slipping inside the scrap of lace at her hips, she murmured, "You first."

He removed his hands and dropped his drawers. But he was back in position before she even had a chance to take a look.

She whispered, "That's not fair. Maybe I want to refresh my memory too."

He gave a strangled laugh. "You may not do that for a bit," he said. "As you stand here before me, I realize how much I've forgotten, and yet, how much I couldn't forget. And all I want to do is bury myself deep inside."

She moaned as his words rolled over her, dropping to her knees, then collapsing backward on the bed. She raised her arms to him. "Come to me then. I've been empty for far too long."

Slowly he lowered himself to lie down beside her, his fingers gently moving up over her cheeks and her mouth, dropping kisses on her lips, down her neck, then her breastbone, gently taking first one nipple, then the other in his mouth, laving them with his tongue.

She twisted and moaned, whispering, "I've missed you so much."

"And I you," he said, rearing up to kiss her hard, long and deep.

When their tongues slowly separated, she realized he was sliding up and down against her body, his erection prodding her belly and the hollow between her thighs. She lifted her hips, trying to grab him and to hold him tight forever.

He nuzzled the underside of her neck and whispered, "You're still wearing a piece of material."

"Then you should take it off," she said, groaning as he trailed a row of kisses along her belly, down to the curls hidden underneath the scrap of material, his tongue gently seeking and finding the nub between the folds of her skin, the scrap of material somehow mysteriously gone.

He kissed her intimately once, twice, only to replace his lips with his penis as he gently kneeled and lifted her hips higher. He slowly entered, lifting her upright to sit on his knees.

She straightened to wrap her arms around his neck, her lips coming down hard on his.

"Golden girl," he whispered. "What was your favorite hobby growing up?"

Her voice broke as she whispered, "Riding."

"Then ride, beautiful one. Just ride."

As he kneeled, her legs behind him, together they set a motion that reminded her of crossing the meadows with her beautiful mare beneath her thighs, her legs clasping as she stroked up and down, deeper and deeper, the movement increasing as he held her hips and helped her to increase the pace until she cried out. Her body arched back, and still her hips kept moving, pulsating, plunging him deeper and deeper.

When she cried out his name, he whispered, "It's all right, sweetie. I'm here." He leaned forward, taking a nipple in his mouth, sucking deep.

Her belly responded, and way below too. And a heat rose, twisting and twisting, higher and higher, until she climaxed in his arms.

She knew he was watching. He wasn't quite ready. Then he slowly lowered her to the bed and dove in, twisting his hips as he groaned, diving deeper until he was seated right at the entrance to her womb, and she could hear the guttural groan as his own release overwhelmed him.

When he slowly sagged down beside her, she wrapped her arms tightly around him, holding him close.

"Just sleep, sweetie," he whispered. "Just sleep."

She didn't realize how tired she was. But, after this, exhaustion once again rippled through her body, taking her back under to the point of losing control, and, already under, she could hear herself ask, "Are you leaving now?"

He whispered back words to remember, "No. I'm not leaving again."

ZANE HELD HER close in his arms, willing the moment to never end. His answer had been heartfelt, but he also realized it was true. He was done walking away. He was done leaving. Somehow Badger had known this was where he belonged. With her here in Maine, come what may, this would be Zane's home.

He would get resistance from his father and brother. He didn't know if there would be resistance from anybody else. His family hadn't cared about him for a long time. He figured his joy in being with Holly would make up for all of that and much, much more.

It was hard to remember the details of their breakup from a long time ago because that was what it was—a long time ago. They weren't those people anymore. He certainly wasn't that young man. And the fact that they'd found each other at this point in their lives was something extraspecial. He wouldn't begrudge himself this second chance.

He'd spent a lot of years traveling, searching, looking for where he belonged and who he belonged with. He thought he'd found it a couple times, but they'd never been anywhere near as close or as special as Holly was to him. Having her back in his arms was a gift—a gift he had never expected.

He cuddled her close and let her sleep. She needed it. At the same time, he wanted to stay awake and watch over her, just watch her. He loved the way her breasts rose, that small fine-boned chest, in a smooth and even rhythm. The way the breath eased out between those plump lips, the rosy glow on her cheeks.

He leaned over and kissed the cheek closest to him. "I put that there," he whispered more to himself than for her ears. "There is such good between us."

He knew there was a lot of good here. More than to be expected, more than he ever thought he would have found.

He wondered at all the reasons why he had refused to come home and knew none of them were any use anymore. None of them were valid because, once again, he and Holly weren't the same people. He didn't carry the same fears and insecurities he'd had before, and neither did she. She'd put his kid brother into her past, and that was what Zane would do too.

And he'd meant every word he'd said outside.

He lay thinking about his options and what he could do until he heard a noise downstairs. He looked over to see Katch, having rolled over to lie on all fours. His ears pricked up, but he wasn't growling. It was just a noise to him.

Zane slid out of bed and pulled on his boxers and jeans, looking out the window. He couldn't see anything. He walked down the hallway and looked out one of the front windows. And groaned. *Dad, what do you want?*

Zane didn't see his dad leave the vehicle because he was already on his way to the front door. He ran down, hoping he could get the door open before his father knocked and woke up Holly. As he opened the door, it kicked open right in front of him.

He stared at his very drunk, boozy father weaving at the front step. "Dad, what are you doing here?" he snapped.

His father looked at him blurry-eyed and lifted what Zane hadn't seen in his hand before. A sawed-off shotgun.

"Dad, what are you doing?" he cried out, hoping to

reach him through his alcoholic haze.

"Where's that goddamn dog?" he roared.

Zane tried to take the shotgun away, but his father's finger was on the trigger. Any attempt he made to pull it free would make it go off and likely hit him.

"He's responsible for all this. If he's dead, you'll leave, just like you should have never come back."

Dazed and hurt by his father's words, Zane stared into his dad's drunken eyes. "What are you talking about?"

"You came here for the goddamn dog, and you're still here because of the goddamn dog," his father snapped. For being as drunk as he was, his words were incredibly clear. "And you need to leave. The only way you'll leave is if that goddamn dog isn't around for you to look after anymore." He shoved Zane with the butt of the gun. "Now where is he?"

"He's at the clinic," Zane said, improvising. "He's not likely to make it through surgery."

His father froze and stared at him for a long moment, then shook his head. "No, no," he said. "I don't believe you. I spoke this morning to Mittle. She said the dog was doing well."

Inside Zane swore. "Yeah, that was probably yesterday," he said, trying to pacify his father. "We had a really shitty evening last night because somebody came into the clinic and tried to attack the dog."

His father poked him again with the butt of the gun. "You always were one son of a lying bitch," he said.

Zane stared at him, not sure what this side of his father was all about. "Why do you want me to leave so bad?"

"I want you to stop sniffing around your brother's wife," his father said. "It's disgusting."

"Holly?" Zane asked, trying to dampen his own ire. "Have you forgotten? She was my girlfriend for years before she married Brody."

"Don't you say his name," his father yelled. "You've got no business living when he died."

The small part that somehow still held some hope his father loved him just completely shriveled up and died. "I know," he said, his voice going hard. "You always liked Brody more than me. And you hoped with all the years I was in the service, I would have gotten killed. Instead, it was our beloved Brody who died and from a stupid reason like a staph infection. And I know you're overcome with grief, Dad, but this is hardly the way to handle it."

"I'll handle it in any way I want to," he said, roaring.

A voice behind them called out, "Jeffrey, what are you doing here?"

"Go back upstairs," Zane told her. "My dad is here to kill Katch."

Just then Katch hobbled down the stairs and froze, seeing the tableau in front of him. He looked hesitant, not sure where to go.

Holly dropped to the ground in front of Katch, blocking him from Jeffrey's view. "Jeffrey, you've got no business coming in here with a gun." Her voice was surprisingly calm. "I want you to turn around and leave now."

He raised that gun and pointed it at her.

That's when Zane lost it. He slammed his hand up underneath the shotgun, hearing it fire as his father's finger pulled the trigger as a reflex. Thankfully the bullet plowed into the rafters above. Zane took the butt end of the gun and smacked it hard against his father's jaw.

His father looked at him, a wounded look in his eyes as

he fell to his knees, then face-planted hard onto the floor.

With the gun now removed from his hands, Holly ran forward and dropped down beside him. "He's alive," she said, looking over at Zane. "What the hell do we do now?"

He stared down at his father, shaking his head. "We're calling the cops," he said. "This has got to stop."

She reached up a hand, grabbing his. "I'm sorry. I heard what he said."

"It doesn't matter what he said. Call them. My father is a lot of things, but a loving, compassionate man he is not."

While she called 9-1-1, Zane called Butch. When he explained what had happened, Butch started to swear on the other end. "That goddamn fool," he said. "I'm surprised he hasn't killed someone by now."

"Well, he came here attempting to kill a dog," Zane said wearily. "But it's really me he hates. It was me he would have been happy to take down."

Butch hesitated, then said, "I know we've never been close, Zane, but he's not been the same since Brody's death. I don't even have much to do with him. I keep a wary eye on him, knowing he's a time bomb ready to go off because I don't really have a whole lot of choice."

"I know," Zane said. "And I don't hold that against you. He said some pretty hard things to me today, but they're nothing I didn't already know."

"You can't listen to him when he's drunk. You know that." Butch's voice hardened. "Hell, we learned that on his knee. If it wasn't a physical beating, it was a verbal beating, so don't you listen to anything he has to say."

"I needed to let you know I called the cops," Zane said. "Not necessarily my choice, but this has to stop. Next time he won't be coming after the dog. He'll be coming after me."

"He's not likely to be coming after anybody," Holly said.

Zane turned to look down at her. "What are you talking about?"

She studied his father's features. "If I'm not mistaken, your father's a very sick man." She looked up at him. "We need to get him to the hospital."

"Are you saying I did this?" He squatted beside his father.

In his ear his brother said, "You just defended yourself and your family. I'm sorry it had to be the old man who put you in this spot, but you are not to blame."

"Thanks, Butch. I'll try to remember that. I'll let you know how this pans out." He put away his phone, checking his father, seeing the yellowish skin and the cloudy eyes. "I'm not sure what I'm looking at."

"I'm not a people doctor," Holly said, "but I'm guessing, from the color of his skin and his eyeballs, that his liver is in serious trouble. I noticed it a while ago but didn't really recognize what that meant, but the symptoms are prominent now. Then what else could he expect, based on the number of years of alcohol poisoning he has inflicted upon his body?"

"Do you think so?"

"We'll find out once he's at the hospital," she said. "That's where he needs to go. I don't think you did any more damage, but you were like the last straw on a body that has already had way-too-much abuse." She stood and walked out to the front. "I hear the police now."

He reached down and gently stroked his father's cheek. "This is not how I wanted it to end."

"It's not over yet," she said. "He's alive and still breathing. But I think we'll find he's dealing with some major chronic conditions, and that's something he either didn't want to accept, didn't want to acknowledge or had no intention of getting tested for."

"His only goal in life was to die and join our mother—and now Brody," Zane said, "but Dad was too much of a coward. He told me once he was trying to kill himself the easy way."

"Drinking yourself to death is not exactly an easy way." She reached out and squeezed Zane's shoulder. "Step back."

He looked up to find the cops and paramedics were here. They checked his father over and loaded him onto a gurney. Within seconds he was gone.

The same detective from before looked at Holly and then at Zane. "I'm not sure I want to know what happened here."

Instead of Zane having to explain, Holly told him all about it. Zane realized she'd heard basically everything from the moment he'd left her bed.

One of the cops with the detective nodded. He looked over at the dog and said, "Katch, you sure are a pile of trouble."

He hopped up to his feet and, moving slowly and painfully, came over toward Zane for a bit of a cuddle.

"It's called misplaced anger," the other cop said, chuckling. "The dog didn't do anything. But, once again, he was picked on by somebody who couldn't deal with his own pain. We're going to take off. We promise we won't be back until tomorrow for your statement on the other case. You guys need to rest up and maybe keep all your family away from here for a while." And they closed the door.

Holly looked at Zane and asked, "Do you want to go to the hospital?"

"No," he said, "but I'll call. I think they'll need to run a bunch of tests." He put in a phone call, explaining his father was coming by ambulance and to have somebody contact him when they had the test results. He said, "I suggest we take a fresh cup of coffee outside and sit in the sunshine and remember all the good things instead of the bad."

She smiled. "I haven't heard a better suggestion, at least in the last hour." She gave him a cheeky grin, and the three of them strolled outside.

They didn't have to wait long before the doctor called him back. "We don't need to run too many tests. It's all in his file. Your dad's liver is pretty well done for. He was given a prognosis of less than three months to live, and that was five months ago. I wouldn't be at all surprised if he isn't gone within a week or two. He is weak. If you want to come in and make peace with him, I suggest you do it now."

"No," Zane said. "I already made peace with him. Let me know what his condition is tomorrow, and we'll see if we can get him back home again."

"I doubt that'll happen," the doctor warned. "I highly suspect he'll go to a hospice."

"If that's the way it is," Zane said, wrapping his arm around Holly, "then that's the way it is. Thanks for the call, Doctor."

She reached up and placed a finger over his lips when he put the phone on the bench. "It's not your fault."

He looked at her, and his smile warmed. "No," he said, "it isn't. This is his fault entirely. I'm just sad for such a wasted life."

She wrapped her arms around his neck and whispered, "So let's not waste ours, okay?"

"Okay," he whispered, kissing her and tugging her gently onto his lap. Together they sat for a long moment, enjoying the sunshine of the afternoon and each other.

EPILOGUE

J AGER WALKED INTO the boardroom to fill his cup of coffee. "Who decided the coffeemaker should be in here anyway?"

At the odd silence, he turned around to see Blaze Bingham sitting at the boardroom table, a guilty look on his face.

Jager raised an eyebrow. "The least you could do is answer," he said jokingly.

Blaze grinned at him, putting photographs together into a stack. "Personally I think it's a silly place for the coffeemaker, but, when you get a cup of coffee and turn around, you see this big empty table. It does invite all kinds of things." He motioned at his own cup. "Which is why I haven't left yet."

"You're done for the day anyway, aren't you?" Jager asked, sitting down at the table, studying the man in front of him. He had a scar across his cheek that twisted his features somewhat, but he was still a good-looking man. The scar gave him a badass look. Jager imagined the women would like it, if they ever got past the initial shock. But then again Blaze, it appeared, deliberately kept himself out of the social scene. Jager wondered at that, but then they all had their own challenges when it came to getting back into the circle of life after recovering from an extreme injury. "What are all those photos?"

Blaze just chuckled, spreading them out before him. "Most people have pictures of babies," he said. "These are my babies. I volunteer at the local rescue center."

Jager looked down and saw dogs, more dogs and even more dogs. He smiled as he picked up one of a French bulldog, his grin wide and happy. "These are all at the shelter?" he questioned. "I hope not because that would mean the shelter is incredibly full of unwanted animals."

"No," Blaze said. "These are the ones we've helped place. Rescuing animals is good for the soul."

"Do you have much dog training?" He studied Blaze's face intently. They still needed more men for the K9 files. They had three down, all successful, and he didn't want to slow the momentum now. But every one of the men had gone out, and not one of them had come back. Personally Jager thought that made it a double success, but he wasn't so sure the commander who'd placed his trust in the Titanium Corp and the rest of the guys here would agree.

"I grew up raising them," Blaze said. "My dad is crazy for Newfies and Saint Bernards. We had purebreds. My mom used to show them, and Dad raised and trained them."

"So you have some training experience?"

"Some," he said. "My dad is a wicked hand at that though."

"I'm surprised you didn't go into the K9 unit in the military then."

"I tried," Blaze said, giving him a lopsided grin. "But I failed."

At that, Jager's eyebrows shot up. "It doesn't look to me like you failed at much in life."

"I'd like to think I failed at this one for the right reasons."

Jager waited.

Blaze reached down, picked up a photo, then slowly brought it to him, then stacking them all together again. "Part of the reason those particular dogs were in the military is for the grueling training they go through. But trainers and handlers are warned that we're not allowed to get too attached. We're told these dogs could move out, not become part of the group and that we wouldn't have any say in the matter. We'd be handlers, not owners. Now, if we retired and the dog was retiring at the same time, maybe. But ..."

"You figured you couldn't go into it without your heart getting engaged."

"Absolutely," he said.

"Interesting. How do you like working here?"

"To be honest," he said, "it's just a stopgap measure. I was thinking about going home to my dad, maybe taking over the family business."

"Training Saint Bernards and Newfies?"

"Maybe other dogs," Blaze said. "The old man keeps telling me to come back. We lost Mom two years back, and he's lonely. There's just him and me now."

"Where's home?"

"Kentucky," he said.

"You're here in New Mexico. Why?"

"Because I was still wandering my way back there. It seems like I was doing everything I could to avoid going home. Going home triumphant after a promotion or willingly retiring from a long and illustrious career is one thing. Going home broken and not quite yourself is a completely different thing."

"How serious were the injuries?"

He shrugged. "Compared to you guys? I'm probably not

too bad. I have a prosthetic foot, missing a rib on the right, lost a little off the liver, and my spleen is gone."

"All survivable injuries," Jager said, knowing just how tough those recoveries would have been.

"Absolutely," Blaze said. "Which is why I'm sitting here now. I want to go home, but I haven't quite adjusted myself to going home as less than I was."

"I don't think you're less," Jager said. "In fact, after all the shit we've been through, I think of us as more. But your focus is on the wrong element. I think it's more about life. We make plans, then life takes you out, blows you up and says, *Okay, so now what are you going to do?*"

Blaze chuckled. "God, isn't that the truth? It's been good for me here—to see everybody's issues, not just my own. The rehab center didn't seem real. Everybody had such major traumas that I could almost disassociate from it, believe I was doing better. That, as long as I ignored it, I was still better off than everybody around me, and so I could return to a normal life. But, of course, the reality is, this *is* a normal life, but it's not the same one I left."

"You have to be adaptable," Jager said.

"And you're not the first one to tell me that," Blaze said. "You see? Each of you guys, you've all found partners. You've all got prosthetics of one kind or another, injuries that I'm sure go well beneath the skin, and yet, you've all done very well for yourselves."

"I think a large part of that," Jager said in all seriousness, "is the support group we have around us. I had these guys with me. They're the ones who helped me pull through. And even though I went ... I'll use the word *dark* for the sake of understanding at the moment ... I walked away from everything and everyone. When it was time to come back to the light, I came back to these guys because I knew they understood. I knew they were where I needed to be. And I knew if I had any way at all to make it happen, I needed to stay close."

"That's because you were all in the same unit," Blaze said. "And I understand that. I wish I had that, but I don't."

"No," Jager said, "but you have something else many of us don't have, and I think many of us would almost take over what we do have. I say *almost* because the bonds between us are very, very tight. But you have a father—a father who loves you, a father who's willing to give you some training, a second chance, his time and energy. You don't know how much longer you have him around to volunteer that."

"Exactly why I'm sitting here going over these photos," he said. "These are successes in the sense that these are rescues that came in, were rehabilitated and moved on."

Jager waited, knowing that Blaze's next line was the one that really counted.

Blaze lifted his gaze, stared at Jager, and once again that crooked smile peeked out. "I came here broken, not connected to who I really was. I feel like I'm rehabilitated and that it's time to move on."

"If you're interested," Jager said, "I have a way for you to go home that maybe won't feel like you're returning with your tail between your legs."

Blaze studied him, an eyebrow raising. "You're offering me a job back home? I don't know how that would work."

"It's not so much a job as a mission from Commander Cross."

At that, Blaze sat back and said, "Wow. That's not a name I've heard very often."

"No. He requested our assistance with a program that got shut down, and of course, typical of all programs, the chances of it being reopened are pretty nonexistent. He asked us to finish what the department had been working on when they lost their budget funding and their staff."

"Okay. I'm confused," Blaze said. He reached forward, grabbed his cup of coffee and took a big sip, his gaze never leaving Jager's. "Tell me more. I'm not exactly sure what you're talking about."

Jager explained as much as he could. "I can't guarantee that the dog," Jager continued, "is still in Kentucky, but I do recall one of them was last seen there."

"Not only might it not be there," Blaze warned, "it could be anywhere by now."

"Exactly. However, our intel so far has been spot-on with the last three War Dogs."

"Interesting, and what am I supposed to do when I find this missing female shepherd?"

"Consider this a welfare check," Jager said. "Make sure she's okay, in good hands and living a decent life."

"Easy to do, if she is in a good situation. But what if she's not?"

"Which is why we're even more concerned about following up on these animals as soon as we can," Jaeger admitted. "The first three were not in ideal situations. In each case though, they ended up in the very best scenario."

"What?" Blaze said. "The men adopted them themselves?"

Jager chuckled. "In two cases, yes. Ethan has Sentry, but he also gained three more with a fourth on the way. I believe he is now doing training workshops, training the animals to be taken out in various situations."

"Wow, good for him. But then Ethan was a K9 handler, wasn't he?"

"K9 handler and trainer," Jager confirmed. "Pierce, … well, he helped reunite his lost dog with her owner before she was shot."

"That's just wrong," Blaze said stoutly. "These dogs have served their country many times over. Why would anybody want to do that to them?"

"It's a tough thing to understand. The third one was Zane back to his hometown in Maine. He found his dog, called Katch, literally being hunted. He caught up to him at a vet clinic, and, meanwhile, Zane went back to an ex-girlfriend, and the two of them are together again, and he has adopted Katch."

"I'm not going home to an ex-girlfriend," Blaze said, "so that won't work."

"You might be surprised," Jager said. "Consider this. We don't know who or what or why we're directed to certain places, but, if we leave ourselves open to what may come," he spoke with a big grin, "just look at us. We all arrived here without partners. And we're now seven married men who couldn't be happier."

"I could hope for something like that," Blaze said, unconsciously stroking the scar on his cheek, "but I highly doubt that'll happen."

"We thought the same thing," Jager said with a nod. "Don't listen to that voice. That's fear talking. Fear that you'll be alone, fear that nobody will see past the scars. And it's not true. You've got seven prime examples right here in front of you. We found unbelievably wonderful women who could see so much more than what we saw in ourselves."

"Sure. But now you're adding a dog to the package."

Jager stood and grinned. "Dogs are supposed to be chick magnets. Remember?"

"Ah, so that's what you're doing. You're throwing me a bone, literally, to help me get a partner." Blaze shook his head. "There's got to be somebody better for this job."

"Maybe," Jager said. "In which case, we'll offer him one of the other missing dog files." Then he added, "Besides, how many of us have families who train animals? How many of us have families and properties that can handle a K9 animal that just wants to come home and rest? Remember she has her own scars, and she's just looking for love too."

And, with that, Jager walked out, leaving Blaze wondering what he'd just signed up for.

This concludes Book 3 of The K9 Files: Zane.
Read about Blaze: The K9 Files, Book 4

THE K9 FILES: BLAZE (BOOK #4)

Blaze had planned to go home to Rockfield, Kentucky, some day. He just hadn't expected it to be this soon ...

Until Badger offers a reason to head in that direction. As a longtime animal-rescue volunteer, hearing about the plight of Solo, a shepherd with severe dissociative issues from her military days, Blaze knows he has to see this through.

Camilla, on her way to an event she's planning, tries to avoid hitting a dog as it runs across the road. Blaze witnesses the accident and stops to help, realizing this could be the shepherd he's looking for. Even better, Camilla is a hoot, and it's been so long since Blaze has had anything to smile about.

But memories run long and insults cut deep, and someone isn't happy about their blossoming friendship. Or maybe even several someones ... How far will they go to stop it? And who will still be standing when this all ends?

Book 4 is available now!

To find out more visit Dale Mayer's website.

http://smarturl.it/BlazeDMUniversal

Author's Note

Thank you for reading Zane: The K9 Files, Book 3! If you enjoyed the book, please take a moment and leave a short review.

Dear reader,

I love to hear from readers, and you can contact me at my website: www.dalemayer.com or at my Facebook author page. To be informed of new releases and special offers, sign up for my newsletter or follow me on BookBub. And if you are interested in joining Dale Mayer's Reader Group, here is the Facebook sign up page.
facebook.com/groups/402384989872660

Cheers,
Dale Mayer

Get THREE Free Books Now!

Have you met the SEALS of Honor?

SEALs of Honor Books 1, 2, and 3. Follow the stories of brave, badass warriors who serve their country with honor and love their women to the limits of life and death.

Read Mason, Hawk, and Dane right now for FREE.

Go here and tell me where to send them!
http://smarturl.it/EthanBofB

About the Author

Dale Mayer is a USA Today bestselling author best known for her Psychic Visions and Family Blood Ties series. Her contemporary romances are raw and full of passion and emotion (Second Chances, SKIN), her thrillers will keep you guessing (By Death series), and her romantic comedies will keep you giggling (It's a Dog's Life and Charmin Marvin Romantic Comedy series).

She honors the stories that come to her – and some of them are crazy and break all the rules and cross multiple genres!

To go with her fiction, she also writes nonfiction in many different fields with books available on resume writing, companion gardening and the US mortgage system. She has recently published her Career Essentials Series. All her books are available in print and ebook format.

Connect with Dale Mayer Online

Dale's Website – www.dalemayer.com
Twitter – @DaleMayer
Facebook – dalemayer.com/fb
BookBub – bookbub.com/authors/dale-mayer

Also by Dale Mayer

Published Adult Books:

The K9 Files
Ethan, Book 1
Pierce, Book 2
Zane, Book 3
Blaze, Book 4
Lucas, Book 5
Parker, Book 6
Carter, Book 7

Lovely Lethal Gardens
Arsenic in the Azaleas, Book 1
Bones in the Begonias, Book 2
Corpse in the Carnations, Book 3
Daggers in the Dahlias, Book 4
Evidence in the Echinacea, Book 5
Footprints in the Ferns, Book 6

Psychic Vision Series
Tuesday's Child
Hide 'n Go Seek
Maddy's Floor
Garden of Sorrow
Knock Knock...
Rare Find

Eyes to the Soul
Now You See Her
Shattered
Into the Abyss
Seeds of Malice
Eye of the Falcon
Itsy-Bitsy Spider
Unmasked
Deep Beneath
Psychic Visions Books 1–3
Psychic Visions Books 4–6
Psychic Visions Books 7–9

By Death Series
Touched by Death
Haunted by Death
Chilled by Death
By Death Books 1–3

Broken Protocols – Romantic Comedy Series
Cat's Meow
Cat's Pajamas
Cat's Cradle
Cat's Claus
Broken Protocols 1-4

Broken and... Mending
Skin
Scars
Scales (of Justice)
Broken but... Mending 1-3

Glory

Genesis

Tori

Celeste

Glory Trilogy

Biker Blues

Morgan: Biker Blues, Volume 1

Cash: Biker Blues, Volume 2

SEALs of Honor

Mason: SEALs of Honor, Book 1

Hawk: SEALs of Honor, Book 2

Dane: SEALs of Honor, Book 3

Swede: SEALs of Honor, Book 4

Shadow: SEALs of Honor, Book 5

Cooper: SEALs of Honor, Book 6

Markus: SEALs of Honor, Book 7

Evan: SEALs of Honor, Book 8

Mason's Wish: SEALs of Honor, Book 9

Chase: SEALs of Honor, Book 10

Brett: SEALs of Honor, Book 11

Devlin: SEALs of Honor, Book 12

Easton: SEALs of Honor, Book 13

Ryder: SEALs of Honor, Book 14

Macklin: SEALs of Honor, Book 15

Corey: SEALs of Honor, Book 16

Warrick: SEALs of Honor, Book 17

Tanner: SEALs of Honor, Book 18

Jackson: SEALs of Honor, Book 19

Kanen: SEALs of Honor, Book 20

Nelson: SEALs of Honor, Book 21

Heroes for Hire, Books 13–15

SEALs of Steel
Badger: SEALs of Steel, Book 1
Erick: SEALs of Steel, Book 2
Cade: SEALs of Steel, Book 3
Talon: SEALs of Steel, Book 4
Laszlo: SEALs of Steel, Book 5
Geir: SEALs of Steel, Book 6
Jager: SEALs of Steel, Book 7
The Final Reveal: SEALs of Steel, Book 8
SEALs of Steel, Books 1–4
SEALs of Steel, Books 5–8
SEALs of Steel, Books 1–8

Collections
Dare to Be You...
Dare to Love...
Dare to be Strong...
RomanceX3

Standalone Novellas
It's a Dog's Life
Riana's Revenge
Second Chances

Published Young Adult Books:

Family Blood Ties Series
Vampire in Denial
Vampire in Distress
Vampire in Design

Vampire in Deceit

Vampire in Defiance

Vampire in Conflict

Vampire in Chaos

Vampire in Crisis

Vampire in Control

Vampire in Charge

Family Blood Ties Set 1–3

Family Blood Ties Set 1–5

Family Blood Ties Set 4–6

Family Blood Ties Set 7–9

Sian's Solution, A Family Blood Ties Series Prequel
Novelette

Design series

Dangerous Designs

Deadly Designs

Darkest Designs

Design Series Trilogy

Standalone

In Cassie's Corner

Gem Stone (a Gemma Stone Mystery)

Time Thieves

Published Non-Fiction Books:

Career Essentials

Career Essentials: The Résumé

Career Essentials: The Cover Letter

Career Essentials: The Interview

Career Essentials: 3 in 1

Printed in Poland
by Amazon Fulfillment
Poland Sp. z o.o., Wrocław

57583434R00128